D1105144

The Killer Breath

By John Wyllie:

THE KILLER BREATH
A POCKET FULL OF DEAD
DEATH IS A DRUM . . . BEATING FOREVER
TO CATCH A VIPER
THE BUTTERFLY FLOOD
SKULL STILL BONE
THE GOODLY SEED
DOWN WILL COME THE SKY
RIOT
JOHNNY PURPLE

The Killer Breath

JOHN WYLLIE

PUBLISHED FOR THE CRIME CLUB BY

DOUBLEDAY & COMPANY, INC.

GARDEN CITY, NEW YORK

1979

All of the characters in this book
are fictitious, and any resemblance
to actual persons, living or dead,
is purely coincidental.

ISBN: 0-385-15204-3
Library of Congress Catalog Card Number 78–22622
Copyright © 1979 by John Wyllie
All Rights Reserved
Printed in the United States of America
First Edition

Pour la belle Nicole

The Killer Breath

CHAPTER ONE

"That's a job for the police . . ."

Through a window in his consulting room Doctor Quarshie could see a tree lizard. It could have been a miniature dinosaur with its green body, bright orange head, tail tipped with orange and black and heavy, scaly ridge which grew over its skull and down its back. It kept making aggressive press-ups, seemingly in defiance of the humid expanse of white sand around it.

The heat made every movement an effort. It was near the end of the rainy season and moisture seemed to impregnate everything, so that people felt as if they were walking around wrapped in a coating of hot, wet jersey.

Perhaps it was something to do with the weather, Quarshie thought, that was responsible for the fact that when he had asked the patient he was examining to take off her clothes she had dropped them swiftly where she stood as if she were glad to be rid of them.

Now she lay on her face on the couch and she was so fat that she had dimples on her shoulder blades and her buttocks were so pitted that they appeared to be covered with many small thumbprints.

Lowering the ear tubes of his stethoscope and hooking them around the back of his neck, Quarshie told her, "You can dress. Then come and sit over here." He indicated a chair in front of his desk and wondered, as the Honourable Mrs. Artson-Eskill Q.C. heaved her massive flesh off the couch, what the prisoners whom she confronted in court would feel if they could see her in her present state. She had a reputation for being able to strike terror into them. Would they laugh if they could see her as he was seeing her, or would they be even more terrified?

In the nude Akhana's leading female barrister-at-law and state prosecutor looked like a figure assembled from an assortment of inflated balloons, with her joints marked at the points at which the balloons were closed off to prevent air escaping and then tied closely together to form a human figure.

Her cheeks pinched her lips between them like a pair of sausages between the sides of two pumpkins. She was heavily made up and her large dark eyes were painted into her face inside circles of blue eye shadow. Conceding that African males liked their women fat, Quarshie could not help feeling that she had gone a little too far in an attempt to satisfy their tastes.

It took his patient very little longer to dress than it had to undress. She had only to pull on an enormous pair of briefs, don a brassière and a simple white blouse and with a few well-practiced movements wind a couple of brightly coloured cloths around her waist and over her shoulder and she was ready to continue the consultation. At no time had she removed the brilliant silk head-tie. It was fastened so that its ends hovered above her face like the wings of a gaily painted butterfly.

As she sat down she asked, "Well, Doctor?"

"Physically you are about as healthy as anyone could expect to be and carry the weight you do, though your blood pressure is rather high."

Mrs. Artson-Eskill nodded her head severely. "You are not the first doctor to tell me that." She frowned, made a great effort and then threw five words at him. "Doctor, my daughter has disappeared."

Quarshie said, "I see," noncommittally. He might have added, "We are, at last, getting to the purpose of your visit." Instead he waited for his client—he assumed she was no longer his patient—to continue.

"That's really why I came to see you."

Though she paused expectantly, Quarshie did not respond.

"Will you try to find her?"

"That's a job for the police, isn't it?"

Mrs. Artson-Eskill raised and dropped her huge shoulders a fraction of an inch.

"When you have attended court as often as I have, you learn that the police have the same human frailties as the rest of society and that their principal technique is to ask so many questions that, by the law of averages, they must eventually get a few correct answers. Unfortunately, they too seldom have the imagination to ask the right questions. Also, as we all know, they get paid by unscrupulous reporters to divulge information that can be used to start scandals."

"If I take the job and I ask the right questions, will you answer them?"

After a barely discernable hesitation Mrs. Artson-Eskill replied, "I will do the best I can and"—she paused to give emphasis to the last word and then repeated it—". . . and I am prepared to pay you well. Of course you will work on your own, and everything you say and do will require great circumspection. I have come to you because I know you will respect the fact that anything you discover must be held in the strictest confidence. Also, during your investigations you will never mention my name. Do I make myself clear?"

Quarshie shook his head. "I shall not be working on my own. My wife works with me on every case I undertake."

"Unless I am misinformed," Mrs. Artson-Eskill said, "that is less than the exact truth."

"You *are* misinformed. Once, and only once, I worked alone. Now Mrs. Quarshie works with me on every case, and if you seriously want us to help you I will invite her in, now, so that she can hear whatever else it is that you have to tell me."

"But I don't want her involved in my affairs," Mrs. Artson-Eskill said emphatically. The butterfly wings over her forehead quivered with her indignation. "I don't have much faith in other women's capabilities, Doctor. They are all busybodies and chatterboxes."

"I see. Then all I can do is to prescribe something that will help to reduce your blood pressure and give you the name of a young man who will, I believe, be discreet and may well find the girl for you. That is, if you don't decide, in the end, to do the sensible thing and go to the police." Quarshie pulled his prescription pad towards him and began to uncap his pen.

Mrs. Artson-Eskill made a quick decision. "All right, Doctor, call your wife. I know you are an honourable and responsible man, and I shall expect her to behave in the same way. I only want to be sure that there are no careless strangers meddling in my affairs."

Quarshie met her glance across his desk and held it coolly as he said, "You are certain that you have no objection to Mrs. Quarshie joining me in the search?"

"I have heard that she is a very able woman. If you will vouch for her discretion and assure me that she will differentiate between what she needs to know to help you find my daughter and what she would like to find out to satisfy her female curiosity I am sure she will be quite acceptable."

"No." Quarshie shook his head. "That is not the answer I want. Of course she will be discreet, but you must understand that the need for us to ask the right questions may sometimes make our behaviour seem most intrusive."

"You sound as if you are still trying to put me off, Doctor. Or at least trying to make things as difficult for me as you can."

"Better now than later, Mrs. Artson-Eskill. I also think that you should understand that I don't have any need for your money except to finance my work here. So when you talk of paying well you are talking of paying me to help those who are too poor to afford the expense of proper medical treatment, and not for what I will spend on myself."

Quarshie was sitting erect in his chair, suppressing an acute sense of hostility.

His client gazed down at a gold ring which seemed to be embedded in the flesh of one of her fingers. After a long, thoughtful silence she looked up at the doctor and said, "Call your wife, please. And let us agree to trust each other to do what is best for both our own and our mutual interests. Call your wife and let's get down to business."

Know that there is an unforgivable, total, superlative wickedness which can infect a man to the very essence of his being. It is a contagion . . .

CHAPTER TWO

"They kill often, but never quickly."

Quarshie was in his workshop smoothing the curves in a piece of fine ebony. His carving was an occupation which, when it went well, provided him with a sense of satisfaction that filled him to the tips of his fingers and to the ends of his toes.

There was laughter outside the door and Mrs. Quarshie came into the room, followed by their son, Arimi, and an old family friend, Jules, the French Ambassador to Akhana.

"Well, we've got it all arranged," Mrs. Quarshie announced. "During the holiday Arimi will work three hours a day at the Embassy so that he will have French as well as English when he starts his advanced studies."

Quarshie smiled. "You'll keep him in order, Jules, eh?"

The old man nodded his white head, put his arm around the boy's shoulder and replied, "Maybe we jus' keep him and forget about the order, no? I will tell everyone he is my gran'son and that the beautiful Madame Quarshie is my daughter. You think they will believe me, Arimi?"

"I am an adopted son, sir. Perhaps I could be an adopted grandson."

"*Parfait.* And your adopted mother could be my adopted daughter, which would all be ver' nice. What 'ave you been making, Quarshie?"

Mrs. Quarshie ran a delicately shaped finger over one of the curves in her husband's sculpture and said, "It's beautiful. I would like to know what it is, Quarshie."

"But you've just said what it is."

"What? What did I say it was?"

"Beautiful. Does it have to be something else as well?"

"Yes. I like things and . . . and people . . . to be recognisable."

Quarshie grinned and asked, "You're not speaking of Mrs. Artson-Eskill, by any chance?"

"Of course. I was just telling Jules about her. He says she is a very prominent citizen."

Quarshie let the column of his carving slide through his enormous hand and replied:

"I hear she may be sent as our next Ambassador to the United Nations. Is that true, Jules?"

The old man was the dean of the diplomatic corps in Port St. Mary and had refused several times to take an appointment in any other country. He not only knew more about the history of West Africa than any other white man in the region but he also had contacts who kept him informed about the intentions of many of the governments. This enabled him to forecast their actions almost before their ministers had reached the stage of drawing up their orders.

He nodded. "It is not confirmed, but there is a good chance that it will be. Madame Artson-Eskill is one of my *protégées*. I made the original arrangements for her to study in France eighteen years ago."

"Why?" Quarshie wanted to know, "I mean, why were you interested in her?"

"She was a brilliant student. Bilingual in English and French, as you are, and the daughter of a very, very important family politically. Her great-great-grandfather was the paramount chief of the Miwi people and the last man to rule an empire in this part of the world except for the Ashantihene."

"So she comes from a country of warrior women and all that?" Mrs. Quarshie asked.

"Especially 'all that,' chère madame. At the time when her great-great-gran'father was the big chief, the women there were very powerful, you know? Led by the Queen Mother—Mrs. Artson-Eskill's great-great-gran'mother—the older women were in charge of the family tombs, which make them, at that time, *responsable* for the 'istory of their people. And it is also their business, a very big business, to keep all the census information that is use for tax assessment . . . No one in the realm except the royal women were allow to count the census pebble, all the little stone each village send in because everybody is drop one each in a pot.

"And then the young *demoiselles* of the royal household, wives and daughters, the King had many wives, are given as *filles de joie*—er, how you call it, Quarshie?"

"Mistresses."

"*Oui*, mistress to all the number-one civil and military figure in the nation. This way the King have many, many sharp ears working for him, picking up rumour and intelligence information. So the women hold key position in the government in, number one, recording and interpreting the history and tradition of their society, number two, the control of taxes through the control of the census and number three, as the secret service. Also, as you say already, Prudence, there are many battalion of women in the army, and their reputation is that they are very, very bloody. They kill often, but never quickly."

"And it is one of their descendents that I now have as a client," Quarshie said unhappily. "Why don't I follow my instinct and leave the case alone?"

"Because the money is good," his wife told him, "because we need a new steriliser and because we can beat her at any game she likes to play."

"What about her position now?" Quarshie wanted to know.

"She make a lot of money in the courts. Also I am told she invest her capital very cleverly. She has a very big house up on the edge of the Anhuri plateau with a very big chicken farm. She has hundreds of women to sell her egg for her. She has many car to distribute her egg to many market and everybody detest her. She is— how you say?—*putain,* bitch . . . clevair, clevair bitch."

Quarshie frowned. "The thing I find most peculiar is that she told us that her daughter disappeared over a week ago and yet only today did she make any move to find her."

Mrs. Quarshie said forcibly, "I don't trust her. She knows a lot more than she will talk about. If she told us everything she knows, now, we would get the answers much more quickly. So why doesn't she do that?"

"Because legal people know better than others the wisdom of silence if there is a possibility of their being mixed up in something suspicious," Quarshie told his wife.

"But she would save much time and money—"

Arimi said, "Sir, it's her money she is spending. Isn't it better she puts lots of money into your clinic than into some other sort of thing?"

The Ambassador cried, "Bravo! It is well said. If you tell me things like that at the Embassy, I shall put you on the payroll. So what is your next step, Quarshie?"

"I have delegated it to Mrs. Quarshie. The little town, Adaja, where Mrs. Artson-Eskill has her home, is served by a midwife whom Prudence tutored. She is going up there tomorrow to visit her pupil, to take a look around, to hear what people are talking about and to find out what they know about the missing daughter, Grace, and whether she and her great big mama get along well together."

The Ambassador opened his eyes wide and asked, "From the way that you say that, should I understand that you are thinking she might have got rid of her own flesh and blood?"

Quarshie shrugged and went back to his sandpapering. After a few moments he said, "She frightens me." Then squinting at his carving through half-closed eyes, he added, "But then I always get frightened when I look into anyone's eyes and find that they are full of fear."

CHAPTER THREE

"You can't make sauce without peppers."

Mrs. Quarshie carefully negotiated curve after curve as she drove her car over the snaking, twisting road up the scarp to Adaja. The town stood on the edge of a plateau and had a distant view, across the coastal plain, of the ocean.

Half a dozen times overloaded trucks and buses, swinging wildly on the corners as they plunged downwards, almost forced her into the cliffside, and twice she swore robustly at the drivers in the rough language of the Port St. Mary slums. They did not frighten her, but their reckless driving made her fiercely scornful of the childish machismo that caused them to endanger so heedlessly the lives of other people.

The road she was following was the main highway north out of Port St. Mary and it provided Adaja, when she got there, with its only paved street—though the edges of the tarmac were eaten away so badly that they looked as if they had been cut with a pair of blunt pinking scissors. On each side of these roughly scalloped verges there were deep monsoon gutters.

The houses fronting the road on each side had to be entered across the gutters over small bridges that led to each front door. Without exception the single-storied houses were tarred halfway up their walls. Above that, beneath wide eaves of corrugated iron roofs, their fronts were whitewashed. They presented the viewer with a model of simple perspective as the road narrowed into the distance, flanked on each side by the black and white ribbons of the housefronts.

Cautiously Mrs. Quarshie turned her car into one of the wide dirt roads which branched off the highway. Here the surface of the road was laterite—red, muddy and full of potholes. Here, too, just behind the precision of the houses bordering the highway, the buildings recalled the original township before the British had driven the main road through it in an uncompromisingly straight line.

The style of these houses was much more varied. Some had thatched roofs and mud-walled compounds, others were of painted and sometimes unpainted cinder blocks, while there were a few, a very few, that had grown to have a second story or were waiting to have one constructed and had square reenforced concrete pillars sticking up like candles on a birthday cake.

The midwife's house was a recently built cinder block building, and the cries which greeted Mrs. Quarshie on the threshold suggested that she might have been a much loved member of the family who had returned to her ancestral hearth unexpectedly.

Over and over again Edwia, the young midwife, repeated, "You are welcome, modda, you are welcome." And an old crone, the midwife's mother, was servile as she bowed and muttered salutations over Mrs. Quarshie's hand.

A little later, while the old woman squatted in the small courtyard at the back of the house, fanning a coal pot on which she was preparing food suitable to offer so distinguished a guest, Mrs. Quarshie was settled in a hard, wooden chair, with her former pupil squatting beside her.

The chair was really a man's chair, but had been given to Mrs. Quarshie because squatting in her rather tight blue uniform dress, now stained with black patches of sweat under her arms and across her back, would be uncomfortable and would force her to display an immodest view of her plump thighs.

After greetings, gossip and some talk about midwifery, Mrs. Quarshie explained her visit by saying that she was touring the plateau to examine possible sites for setting up extensions to the clinic which her husband ran in Port St. Mary. Then she asked a lot of questions about any similar facilities which already existed in the neighbourhood, the possible attitude of the local people towards a private clinic, the names of the influential people she should talk to and the names of any wealthy citizens in the district who might be prepared to support the clinic.

Mrs. Quarshie heard, as she knew already, that Mrs. Artson-Eskill was the richest person in the neighbourhood and that she was not popular because she was a "foreigner" and behaved in a patronising and autocratic way towards all her neighbours.

And the daughter?

She was not any better liked than her mother. She had, as a young girl, attended the local convent for training in the native religion. There she had flaunted her mother's wealth, power and status to the point where both those who ran the convent and those who attended it were glad to see her leave.

From the convent she had gone on to expensive private schools, first in Akhana and then in Europe. When she came back she behaved as if she had never known any of the people in Adaja and seldom spoke to any of them. Instead, it was said, she spent most of her time talking with students at the University, particularly with those who were known to be troublemakers.

Edwia also reported that one of the women who worked at Mrs. Artson-Eskill's house and was going to have a baby had come to her for an examination. Afterwards, she had told her that there were frequent fights between mother and daughter, and that when they occurred none of the staff at the house, the chicken farm or the factory ever had any sympathy with either of them, and would have been glad to see them destroy each other.

Mrs. Quarshie asked what kind of factory it was.

Patent medicines, they told her. Mrs. Artson-Eskill was in partnership with a local man who bottled and sold traditional herbal remedies. The man was also one of the principals at the convent and famous, locally, as a sorcerer and practitioner of African medicine. He had been trained in England in chemistry but had got into some sort of trouble in Port St. Mary, where he had worked for the government, and had had to return to his family home and profession.

Mrs. Quarshie said, "I would like to see him. He might be a useful man to know."

"Be careful, modda," Edwia told her, "he is a dangerous man."

"In what way dangerous?" Mrs. Quarshie wanted to know.

"He knows white man's medicine and African medicine, and he can use all two to do very bad things."

"What kind of things?"

"Modda, he gave one of my patients medicine to put in another woman's food. My patient was the senior wife of an important man, and she did not want one of the junior wives, her husband's favourite, to have a child. She had already asked me if I could do anything to stop this. Later, the junior wife came to me and was very sick and unhappy. Modda, she was carrying a foetus that was dead."

Mrs. Quarshie looked sympathetic and said the reverse of what she was thinking, "Oh my . . . then you were right, perhaps he is not the kind of man I should contact." It was not the first time that she had heard of a pregnancy being terminated by a sorcerer. Then she added, as if it were an afterthought, "Although I suppose I really should go to see him. The better one knows the people one should fear, the fewer things one finds in them that need to be feared. Also, all men have weaknesses, but you often need to know them well before you can learn enough about their weaknesses to use them."

The man who greeted Mrs. Quarshie, after he had made her wait for over an hour, was as tall as her husband and in a way looked as impressive. The difference between them was that the sorcerer, Julius Asteteompong, appeared to be dressed and even made up to look impressive. Also, Asteteompong's body was shaped like an avocado pear, and Mrs. Quarshie suspected that if someone touched him they would find that the fruit was overripe.

He wore horn-rimmed spectacles, a Western-style suit with a tie, and as he held out his hand he said, "Ah, Mrs. Quarshie. What a pleasure. And to what do I owe the honour of a visit from someone who, I have been told, is an example of just how actively any person can occupy their time?"

Mrs. Quarshie joined the game. She replied, "For my part, I find it amazing that a man like you, with so many important things to occupy his mind, can, at such short notice, spare any time to allow me to sit in this comfortable chair to talk with him."

"You are welcome, most welcome. And what, may I ask, are we to talk about?"

The man's room and his appearance, Mrs. Quarshie decided, mirrored each other. Everything which could give the room identity was concealed. No walls were visible: they were all hidden behind curtains. In some cases it appeared as if there were annexes on the other side of the curtains; elsewhere the drapes had been hung some feet in front of the walls.

Behind his desk there was a window, and Mrs. Quarshie sat facing the light while Asteteompong had his back to it.

He was a fair-complexioned African, though his features were classically negroid. His hair was carefully cut, pomaded and brushed, as were his thick eyebrows. The whites of his eyes glittered faintly blue, and the tip of his nose shone as if it had been polished. His heavy moustache, which drooped around the corners of his mouth, had received the same attention as his eyebrows and hair. Mrs. Quarshie suspected that his lips were stained in some way to give them a more vivid red tone, and though he would have a heavy beard if he allowed it to grow, it had been so closely shaved that his face looked as if it would be as smooth to the touch as doeskin.

Comparing the man for a second time with Quarshie, Mrs. Quarshie decided that her husband's appearance said something about his honesty whereas Asteteompong's spoke only of fraudulence and obliquity. Perhaps, she thought, she was being unfair, but this immaculate man in his carefully planned, noncommittal surroundings radiated vibrations that jarred. Of course, she reminded herself, all this was intuitive. Then she justified her use of intuition by remembering that Quarshie had first been chosen to trace the assassins of a president of Akhana because his sensitivity gave him such a powerful sense of instinct and intuition. Watching him at work over half a dozen cases, she had learned the way to employ intuition.

So far, it seemed, it was not just Mrs. Artson-Eskill whom she distrusted but also those who were closely associated with her, like her daughter, and now this crafty, sleek man who sat opposite to her.

She was troubled, however, that she might not be able to sustain a role in which she had to make certain that any suspicion he might have—and in his work, she thought, he had to be suspicious of everybody—must be anaesthetized if it could not be totally removed.

She said, "I am doing a survey on my husband's behalf. He thinks it would be a good idea to open a clinic here, and I am discussing that idea with all the most important and influential people in the neighbourhood. Naturally, you are one of the first I need to consult. I shall be seeing the Adajamandola, Abuki Dukuwaru the Third, later and of course the District Commissioner, the Bank Manager, the Director of the Medical Authority, Mrs. Artson-Eskill and others, but I thought you would be a good person to start with."
"Don't overdo it, Prudence," she told herself.

"Well now, I have to admit to being flattered, but on what grounds do you place me first?"

Mrs. Quarshie appeared to concentrate hard as she answered, "Well, to begin with, I know that your family has always been a very influential one here, so all levels of the community listen to what you have to say. Also, through your knowledge of African medicine you are a man of the past, and since you have travelled and are a Western-trained pharmacist you are a man of the present. There are very few people here, if there are any, who are so well qualified in both areas.

"Then, of course, your work brings you into contact with almost everybody, rich or poor. So, whom could I find who would be better qualified to know how people would react to the idea of our establishing a clinic here?"

Mr. Asteteompong brushed the corners of his moustache with the forefinger of his right hand, and Mrs. Quarshie noticed that it, too, was plump and looked as if it might bruise easily. In the cool tone of voice that he would use to an inferior he said, "Mrs. Quarshie, or better, Prudence—I have been told that that is your name and I will use it since it seems a fitting one."

Mrs. Quarshie suppressed her reaction to his words with every bit of willpower she possessed. The man was being deliberately impudent. What he was proposing could not have been a greater act of familiarity than if he had tried to put his hand up her skirt. Nobody, but nobody, except her mother, and sometimes Quarshie and the old French Ambassador, ever called her by her first name.

The man paused to see if she would pick up the challenge. When she stared at him grimly but said nothing, he continued, "Prudence, a lot of people come here to sell me things, or to ask me for favours. Often they take a similar approach to the one you have taken. So, now that I have accepted the fact that you want me to do something for you, what are we going to talk about?"

In a voice as cool as his own she told him in detail of Quarshie's plans for the clinic.

Mr. Asteteompong listened without interrupting her. When she had finished he nodded his head gravely and said, very slowly, "Prudence, you did not really have your heart in that statement. Would you like to try again? If you told me your real reasons you might be more convincing."

Mrs. Quarshie felt as if the muscles in her face had frozen. In a voice she did not recognise as her own, a voice in which her feelings had no part, she told him, "I assure you we would like to establish a clinic here but, it is true, I do have other reasons for coming to see you."

And then, while she remained silent, trying to find another way of attacking him, he said, "I'm waiting."

Mrs. Quarshie took a deep breath and with what she felt was considerable conviction because her words were, in fact, heartfelt she said, "Mr. Asteteompong, I am a barren woman. You know the stigma which attaches to that condition in our society. A woman can fail in anything else without being too severely reproached for it, but not that. I want to bear a child, Mr. Asteteompong. You know all the traditional remedies for sterility. Can you help me?"

Mr. Asteteompong's answer again took her aback. "Are you, in your devious way, offering your beautiful self to me, Prudence? Because, as a midwife, you must know that the only proper answer to that question is to be found in bed."

Mrs. Quarshie clenched her hands beneath the desk top in her effort to control her desire to slap his smooth, unctuous face.

In a very still, small voice she said, "I would like the child to be my husband's."

"Ah, I see. And is there anything else you want?"

"Yes. There are two things." Mrs. Quarshie was amazed by her own ready response. "I would like to hear about the cult that you and your family have served for so many years, and I would like to visit the convent which belongs to the cult."

"That's all?"

"Yes."

Mr. Asteteompong thoughtfully cleaned his already immaculate fingernails with the tip of an ivory paper knife while Mrs. Quarshie waited. Now she was quite cool and undisturbed by his obvious wish to make his silence provocative.

Finally, he looked up and said, "I don't know what to think of you, Prudence. We have been playing a game, you and I, haven't we? I am not quite sure what the game is and I don't at this moment want you to tell me because that would take the pleasure out of the challenge it involves. It would be a bit like looking up the answer to a sum in arithmetic before one has arrived at the solution the proper way. I would say that where we stand at the moment is that you don't trust me and I don't trust you." He paused, looking over his spectacles at her, then added, "But I will tell you one thing that you might as well believe because it can do you no harm. I find you a most attractive woman. However, I am no going to ask whether, in this game we are playing, sex is a negotiable element. Though I am going to allow myself the hope that it may be." He sat back and relaxed, folding his hands over his stomach. When he spoke again it was as if his body had been inhabited by another man.

"You asked about the cult my family has served for several generations. I don't need to remind you, I suppose, that our gods were like most other gods in that they ruled over their people and were given two means of ensuring their subjects' obedience—the carrot and the stick, rewards and punishments. My people have two very important gods, the brothers Dagbata and Sevioso. Dagbata, whom my ancestors served, was the god of the earth and everything on it. Sevioso was the god of the air, the sky and the heavens. To gain obedience Dagbata could inflict transgressors with disease. Sevioso, for the same purpose, had thunderbolts.

"Dagbata was the more powerful. His province, the earth, gave men more than Sevioso's; it gave them grain and meat, rivers and forests, mountains and plains, shade and wood to build with and to burn. He also had the most powerful punishment with which to coerce his people: a virulent infection, and he could kill those who were his enemies or those who disobeyed him with it. Sevioso was not, of course, unimportant, because he controlled the weather, the amount of rain that fell and the amount of heat that came from the sun.

"That's all I have time to tell you now: that my family and I serve Dagbata. Another day, when we know each other better, I will tell you more. Or you can come and work at the convent, where you will be taught more. As for paying a visit, that might be inconvenient at the moment. It is better that we warn the staff there before we stroll in because they tend to be hostile to foreigners."

He changed back to his former attitude, sitting forward combatively with his elbows on his desk. "There was that other question, too, wasn't there? You wish to have a child. I can suggest one obvious first step. It is to make sure that the fault is not yours but your husband's by trying the sperm of a number of other men, especially those who have already fathered children, as I have. We servants of

Dagbata do not share the gods' magic powers that would enable us to create life. The only way we can give life, Prudence, is by joining our bodies with those of women. No, we are not creators. But kill we can and do, often, in ways that other men are unable to detect."

In her wraparound African cloth and brightly coloured head-tie Mrs. Quarshie was, from a distance, undistinguishable from the other market women on the road except that she was sitting in her car.

After her interview with Asteteompong she had returned to the home of the young midwife. There she had borrowed the clothes she was now wearing. One asset of the Akhanian style for women's dresses, which are made up of three pieces of uncut cloth, is that there is no problem in making them fit. With her young friend she had taken a sight-seeing trip in the neighbourhood with the purpose of finding Mrs. Artson-Eskill's house but without drawing attention to the fact that this was her objective.

Now, alone, having said her good-byes to her hostess, she had parked in a small lay-by beside the road that was about a hundred yards from the house and enabled her to watch the entrance of the driveway which led up to Mrs. Artson-Eskill's front door.

It was late in the afternoon and the women from the villages around the town were returning from the market carrying empty basins or baskets on their heads if they had been successful in selling their yams, groundnuts, oranges, meat, plantains, corn, kassava, avocados, smoked fish and other produce, or headloading purchases of various other kinds if they had come to the market to buy. There was a continuous stream of them on both sides of the road and they stretched, erect and graceful even when they were carrying heavy items such as sewing machines on their heads, as far as Mrs. Quarshie could see.

Earlier she had been told by Edwia that on market-day evenings Mrs. Artson-Eskill held open house when people could call on her for free legal help, or advice, on any matters that concerned them. Uncharitably, Mrs. Quarshie's informant had also told her that it was the opinion of many people in the town that Mrs. Artson-Eskill's philanthropy was not disinterested. There were, it was said, two reasons for her apparent public-spiritedness. The first was that she could, through her contacts, her wealth and her knowledge of the civil laws of the country do more for people than the Adajamandola, the local Chief, so more people went to her house than to his, for he, too, held court on the same day. So her actions were related to her quest for status and power; she was greedy and determined to outrank the Chief in both.

She also opened her doors so freely because she could elicit all kinds of information from the people who visited her, either without their knowing it or in exchange for her favours and help. What she learned, again, gave her more power, and consequently the ability to manipulate people.

Remembering the conversation she and Quarshie had had with the woman when they first met with her, Mrs. Quarshie could confirm the midwife's statement that Mrs. Artson-Eskill was clever. At that meeting she had told them that she knew nothing about her daughter's disappearance except that she had walked out, without leaving any message, on a market-day evening just over a week ago, and had not returned.

Quarshie had asked her if their relationship had been a good one, and the response had been, as good as most mother-and-daughter relationships.

Had she any idea why Grace might have decided to leave? No, no idea at all. The girl had everything she could possibly want.

Including enough affection?

All things are relative. What is "enough" affection? There were no other people in the family who competed for what she, Mrs. Artson-Eskill, had to give.

And so it had gone on. Her replies had given them nothing tangible to work with.

Of course her daughter was well behaved.

No, they had not had any friends in common. There was thirty years' difference in their ages.

Yes, Grace was competitive; proof of that fact was that she always did well at school.

Men friends? Yes, she had them, though none of them seemed to be very regular, or important.

No, she had never left the house before and failed to come back.

Yes, she had stayed out all night, once or twice. She was, don't forget, over twenty-one.

No, she, Mrs. Artson-Eskill, would not have been upset if she had known it was a man rather than a woman she had stayed with.

And so on, and so on . . .

There was a sudden explosive bang on the roof of the car as if someone had slapped it, and a young woman poked her head through the window and said, "Early tonight?" before she saw who was in the car.

"Oh, sorry, ma," the intruder said quickly, and was about to withdraw her head and walk on when Mrs. Quarshie said, "Yes, I'm early tonight. But I am not sure what I am early for. Here . . ." She put her hand in her purse and pulled out a five-beni note. "Get in the car and talk to me for a few moments. Tell me why I am early."

"I . . . you . . . no be you, ma . . . ee be nodder car, taxi."

"Come on, get in." Mrs. Quarshie reached out and took the girl's hand and pressed the money into it. "I be stranger for here," she told her. "Make you talk small wid me."

Shyly the girl did as she was told, looking around as she did so to see if she was being observed.

There was some anxiety in her voice as she said, "You never go take me someplace, ma?"

"No, I go stop for here. Why you go say I de be early?"

"I tink so dis car belong taxi man come heah every night Adaja day."

The weekdays in the local language were named for the days when markets took place. Every Friday was Adaja.

"Taxi man be frien', nah so?" Mrs. Quarshie asked.

"Small, small, ma."

"He come see you?"

"No, ma. He go bring some man for dis place."

"For what place?"

"Some man he go stop for dissee place dayah." She pointed down the road to Mrs. Artson-Eskill's house.

"Stop long time?"

"Stop long time, ma. Maybe to first cockcrow time."

"An' you de go sit for taxi wid taxi man?"

"Sometime I go sit de heah."

"You de see dis man who come for dissee house how he go look?"

"Yes, ma, I de see him."

"Big man?"

"Yes, ma, big man."

"Young man? Old man?"

"I tink so he de be young. Get big beard, ma. Tink so he de be young behind de beard."

"Taxi from dis place?"

"No, ma. Taxi de be from Port St. Mary."

"You say he de come every Adaja night?"

"E be so, ma. One night he maybe no go come . . . one night, so so in one moon, two moon."

"You get name from dis taxi man?"

"He name Kwadoo, ma."

"He go take you for he house?"

"He say sometime, sometime he de go take me, ma."

"You stay for car wid dis man all night?"

"Sometime I go stay. Sometime I no go stay."

"You tink so you get piccin for dis man?"

The girl giggled but did not reply.

"Dissee Kwadoo he de go tell you som'ting about dissee man he de go bring here."

The girl thought for a minute and then replied:

"One time he go say dissee man catch money too much, ma. Go pay him good for no talk, stay heah dis place wait for um all night."

Mrs. Quarshie hesitated, wondering what else she could ask the girl, but could not think of anything. She wished Quarshie were beside her because she was sure there was something that she had missed.

Her silence made the girl nervous.

"Ma, you no go mak' some bad palaver for me?"

"Why? Why you tink so maybe I mak' bad palaver?"

The girl shook her head dumbly.

Mrs. Quarshie patted her hand and told her, "I no go make bad palaver. Sometime you get trouble, get sick, get piccin, come for Port St. Mary, ax for Doctor Quarshie, den I go help you." And as she said the last word Mrs. Quarshie thought how stupid she was. When someone looked unhappy her instinct to help was too strong. Mrs. Artson-Eskill was not supposed to know that she had been in the neighbourhood. But then, of course, she would know from Asteteompong even if this girl did not talk.

So Mrs. Quarshie shrugged and told herself, "You can't make sauce without peppers." If you wanted answers, you had to ask questions.

She patted the girl's hand again and said, "Make you go now and thank you."

"Yes-em-ma. I de go one time."

The girl paused outside the window and waved to Mrs. Quarshie, flashing the pale palm of her hand.

Mrs. Quarshie returned the wave and started her car.

On the road down the scarp she would be travelling on the outside edge of the road with a drop, from the top, of well over a thousand feet, and she wanted to get that part of the journey behind her before it became dark.

She also wanted to be back with Quarshie because her meeting with Asteteompong had unsettled her and she was not at all sure that she had done a good day's work. She badly needed to feel the reassurance her husband provided when he saw her and his sombre face lit up as he smiled.

CHAPTER FOUR

*"It is a foolish chicken that accepts a
challenge to fight a python."*

Quarshie was driving home from the Akhana State Hospital, where
he served as a consultant. He had been called out after dinner, and
Mrs. Quarshie and Arimi had gone along for the ride.

"So that's the way it is," he said. "It means that I shall be on duty
most of tomorrow. Someone else will have to find Kwadoo, the taxi
driver."

"Me, sir?" enquired Arimi hopefully.

"You, sir," Quarshie confirmed. "Of course I shall be able to help
you, and I will have time to phone Uncle Ezra about Asteteompong. The old man will be able to get hold of his file and
check him out. It's convenient having an uncle who is Permanent
Secretary at Internal Affairs."

"*Sometimes* it's convenient," Mrs. Quarshie corrected her husband. "Sometimes it gets you into a lot of trouble." She was thinking of the occasions when Uncle Ezra had got his nephew involved
in murder hunts—both times had almost cost him his life. "Quarshie, go home along Pagan Road," she added, "I have to buy yams."

Quarshie smiled. "Housewife, midwife and private investigator."

"Do you think that any of the things I told you are going to
help?" Mrs. Quarshie asked, trying, but failing, to restrain a note of
eagerness in her voice.

"We shall soon know. Arimi"—Quarshie spoke over his shoulder
—"in the morning I want you to find a taxi driver named Kolotsi.
He has been in the business longer than anyone else in Port St.
Mary. He will, I think, help us."

"He certainly *should* help us," Mrs. Quarshie corrected him
again. "After all, you saved his son's life."

"Well, yes." Quarshie felt uncomfortable taking credit for something he considered an activity carried out in the line of duty, and continued quickly, "You'll probably find him at the Benin Plaza Hotel waiting to pick up tourists, so you must be there early to catch him before he takes off. Tell him I want to see this Kwadoo and that he drives a taxi which must look a lot like Mrs. Quarshie's car. Then find the man and bring him to the hospital so that I can talk to him. Right?"

"Is that all, sir?" Arimi sounded disappointed.

"It will do to begin with."

Quarshie pulled off the road beside the market.

A large part of the trading area was roofed, but otherwise it was open on all four sides to the night. All the market women lit their baskets or stalls with candles or with wicks floating in shallow saucers of oil or, more infrequently, with hurricane lamps. The market covered more than three acres of ground, and in the dark, with occasional gusts of wind coming in off the sea, it looked as though a gigantic swarm of flickering glowworms had settled there.

Mrs. Quarshie said, "It looks much more exciting now than it does in the daytime."

Her husband grunted and replied, "The sight of a market place has the same effect on most women that the smell of the jungle has on a hunter. I hear they are talking of installing electric lights soon. Big banks of them, for the open areas, like the ones they have at the football stadium."

"Oh, why?" Mrs. Quarshie grieved. "Why can't they leave things alone? And they will probably charge the market women with the cost of the lights, so that all the prices will go up."

Arimi said, "Having floodlights has helped a lot with football. Bigger crowds can attend at night, and the players don't get tired so quickly because it is cooler. Tete is playing tomorrow with the Port St. Mary Tigers. You said once, sir, that you had met him and that you would take me to see him one day."

"Well," Quarshie told Arimi as he and Mrs. Quarshie got out of the car to plunge into the interlocking whirlpools of people packed together in the market, "I'm afraid it won't be tomorrow. I shall be much too busy."

Mr. Kolotsi was a small man with a face shaped like an egg, with its narrowest part upwards, broad in the jowls and almost pointed at the crown of his balding head. The little tufts of hair above his ears were grey, his mouth was wide, his teeth as white as the best bone china and his demeanour jovial.

"You are welcome, my young friend, you are welcome," he informed Arimi when the boy introduced himself. "Come and sit here beside me and tell me your story." And having listened to what Arimi had to say, he told him, "So you want, or rather the great man, your father, wants, to talk with brother Kwadoo, the hairy one. Strong like a gorilla he is. Strong in the arm, strong in his words and strong the gin he drinks. Now, let me see, today is Saturday, no? Perhaps you are lucky. Last night Kwadoo would have been working. This morning he will be home, and except for one, maybe two, bottles of beer, he will not be drinking yet. The big Doctor, I know, drinks beer, too, but not first thing in the morning, eh?"

"And where does Mr. Kwadoo live?"

"Not Mr. Kwadoo, my young friend, but Mr. Lamterry, Kwadoo Lamterry. Wait while I speak small with another driver. He will know the exact place for you to go."

While the man was away talking with his colleague, who was squatting in the shade on the other side of the road, Arimi looked around him.

The hotel, which was eighteen stories high, was the tallest building in Port St. Mary. In front of it, on the terrace, there was a conglomeration of brightly coloured umbrellas. Beneath these there were many people with white skins, and Arimi was surprised at the range and the assortment. Broadly, he realised, they fell into three categories. The tourists had, to an African, either obscenely white skin or skin that was burned by the sun to the disgusting shade of raw meat. Generally, they had unsightly legs, hairy and very short in the shin, which they all insisted on revealing by wearing what Arimi and his friends called "knicker," the kind of small boy's apparel the people of Akhana expected to find being worn by labourers or the poor.

Another category included people with either black or white skins. Obviously they were businessmen, or men who would be dealing with the government. The most fashionable of them wore Senegal suits, a jacket with a shirt-style collar but with no shirt beneath it. The others wore lightweight business suits with ties, and although it was not yet eight o'clock, some of them were already beginning to look hot and uncomfortable.

The final group were young men and women, mostly with their hair long, wearing T-shirts and jeans. It was the latter who most interested Arimi. Nearly all of them were white, and though they were surrounded by much older, more expensively dressed men and women they ignored them, or seemed quite at ease with them. They obviously regarded themselves as free from any kind of constraint or need to show respect for their elders, and he wondered whether he would have the same sort of bearing when he was their age. They also appeared to be bored, and he suspected that was where he would differ from them. Curiosity was something Quarshie constantly tried to stimulate in him.

Mr. Kolotsi came back and directed Arimi to a part of the town mainly inhabited by fishermen.

The inhabitants of Fishermanstown are a people unto themselves. They give the impression that they feel superior to and are independent of the rest of the city. The physical strength of the men is certainly greater, particularly their back, shoulder and arm muscles, features which almost make them look like American footballers with all their protective armour in place. They live on a high-protein diet, never being without fish, and they spend most of their days hauling or setting nets, without shelter from the equatorial sun, in canoes driven by outboard engines.

Visitors to their neighbourhood tread warily, taking care not to give offence or to get involved in any arguments.

Arimi's quarry, Mr. Lamterry, turned out to be a fisherman who had found life less strenuous and perhaps more profitable behind the wheel of a taxi. When the boy moved forward to introduce himself, Kwadoo told him roughly not to disturb him with a "mewing of kittens or whining of puppies."

Arimi retreated a few yards to squat on his heels and to wait. He had not dared to tell Kwadoo, as he wanted to, that he was neither a kitten nor a puppy but the adopted son of Mrs. Quarshie, who was well known in the neighbourhood because she had, at one time, served as its midwife and still came out on calls.

When the man had finished his food and still showed no signs of allowing anyone to disturb him—he had settled on the ground with his feet stretched out in front of him and with his back against the wall of the hut and had closed his eyes—Arimi approached the woman who had served Kwadoo his meal.

Even she was a little timid in her approach to the taxi driver. Kwadoo had discarded his shirt, and Arimi could see why he was called "the hairy one" and "strong." The woman stood out of his reach and spoke very softly to him.

Kwadoo opened one eye and looked at her.

In a voice that was as soft as her own he asked her one or two questions. Then he turned his head and, with both eyes on Arimi, said:

"So you come from the Quarshies?"

"I am their son."

"What do they want of me?"

"My father would like to talk with you."

"Then why doesn't he come to see me?"

"Because he is doing important work at the hospital and cannot get away. He is a pathologist, and with another doctor he is doing some research into lasser fever. They have a case in hospital at the moment, and my father is working on some biopsies of—"

"You use big words, small man, to tell me that I have no book learning. But come here close to me and we will see how much good your books are to you once I have my hands on you."

"It is a foolish chicken that accepts a challenge to fight a python," Arimi said. "But please come, you can help my father a lot."

"He will pay?"

"For your going to the hospital, for any time spent there waiting and for your return here."

Kwadoo called for the woman, and when she came told her, "Give the boy some sugar thing to eat while I bath. I must not visit the Doctor with a whole night's sweat on me."

At the hospital they waited over an hour for Quarshie to be free to see Kwadoo. It was suggested that they wait in the Doctor's office in the pathology building, but Kwadoo would not wait where there was air-conditioning.

"Such things are not the will of Lisa," he said. Lisa is one of the twin gods, the other being Mawu, and they, by one name or another, are accepted in many parts of West Africa as the creators of the world. Lisa, a male divinity, is responsible for sun, power, heat, toughness and labour, and Arimi saw Kwadoo as having a considerable resemblance to him.

So they waited outside in the shade of a mango tree, and Kwadoo, stretched out flat on his back, slept without moving.

The heat came down on them through the overcast sky and the dark green foliage, and it came up at them off the ground in moist waves, carrying with it what Arimi always thought of as the "green smell" (in the dry season it was a "brown smell") of fallen leaves, whether they were mango, rain tree, neem or acacia.

When Quarshie came out he sat with them on the ground under the tree.

He asked Kwadoo, "Do you have any children, friend?"

"I have three," he said.

"A girl amongst them?"

"Yes, one."

"If that girl were to disappear one day how important would it be to you to find her?"

"As important as escaping with my own life if it was threatened."

"That is well said," Quarshie told him, "and it will help you to understand why I want to speak with you."

Kwadoo had produced a rather dry piece of chewing stick from his pocket and was cleaning his teeth with it as he listened.

"A certain woman came to me because she has lost her daughter. Perhaps by answering one or two questions you can help me find the girl."

"I have had nothing to do with the stealing of children."

"I believe you . . . yet it is possible that without knowing it you were very close to such a theft when it happened. Where were you last night and a week ago last night?"

Kwadoo's brows came down together over his eyes, and after he had thought for a moment he said, "To ask that question you must know where I was. So it is no mystery. I was at Adaja."

"And the man you take there: do you know who he is?"

"No."

"What do you know about him?"

"Nothing."

"Does he pay you to know nothing about him?"

"He pays me well and has told me not to talk about him."

"Is the money he pays you more important than finding this woman's daughter?"

"What woman?"

"The woman your passenger goes to see."

Kwadoo made no comment for a while, then he asked, "It is the girl, Grace, you are looking for?"

"It is."

"I can't help you. All I know is what people tell me."

"People? Not a certain young woman who joins you in the taxi while you wait for your passenger?"

Kwadoo seemed to retreat. In a low voice he said, "If you know so much, why bother me with these questions? You have not had someone, this boy, perhaps, following me?"

"What I have told you is all I know. I need to know more. This man, your passenger, he might be important. Who is he?"

"A man with a beard, who never speaks. He wears a small gold chain around one wrist and he smells strongly of foreign perfume."

"I smelled it in your taxi," Arimi said.

Kwadoo nodded. "I had just taken him back to the town."

"So you know where he lives?"

"No. I know where I pick him up. The house belongs to one who takes bets. A fat man who drives a very big car."

"But you don't know anything else about this man? Does he go up to Adaja every week?"

"No, there are some Fridays when he does not go."

"Which Fridays recently did he not go?"

"This week, last week, he went. Before that, one Friday he did not go. Then for three Fridays he went, and before that for two Fridays he did not go. Is it enough? Or should I tell you more?"

"Can you remember that, Arimi?"

"Yes, sir."

"You can show my son the place where this man with the big car lives?"

"I can."

"Good, take him there. That will then be all. Arimi, find out who this man with the beard is." Quarshie took out some money and gave part of it to the driver. "It is enough?"

Kwadoo counted the notes. "It is more than enough," he said. "That much more," and gave two back.

Quarshie shook hands with Kwadoo, and Arimi thought that there was something in the gesture that indicated that the two big men might like to try their strength against each other. He was relieved when they unclasped hands without making any other move.

In the taxi on the way back into town Kwadoo said, "It is good when a man can speak with another and know that they both stand honestly on the same ground." Then he repeated, "Arimi, find out who this man with the beard is." And he laughed. "He thinks well of you, boy. You will grow up like him. Here, in Africa, we need men like Doctor Quarshie, who says truly what he has to say and does not talk with many words when a very few will be enough."

Ten minutes later he stopped the cab and pointed across the street. "That's the house, boy." And he offered his hand to Arimi, saying, "You have a man's head on those small shoulders. Should you need the strength of a man's arm, remember the hairy one, boy. He will help."

The place where the taxi left Arimi was opposite a standpipe, an installation where all those who do not have running water in their houses come to fetch what they need. Many of those who carried water were children, mostly young girls.

Arimi spoke with one of the latter. He asked her, using the same local language that he had used with Kwadoo, "Sister, sometime you can see over there"—he pointed across the street—"a man with a big black beard?"

"I never see anyone so."

"Ask all your friends and family here if they see such a man."

And he repeated this plea over and over again to the people coming for water.

When anyone asked why he wanted to hear about a man with a black beard, he told them it was a part of a holiday task he had been set at school, a test of a student's ability to gather information.

Soon, while he was talking to another girl, he felt a small hand take his elbow. Turning, he found a child of about eight standing close beside him.

She said, "In the nighttime I see a man with a beard come out and get into a car."

Her response gave Arimi an idea for testing the truth of any statements he was offered. He added to his request, "If you saw a man like that what was he doing?" Each time he received what seemed to him to be a likely answer he gave the respondent a beni.

At the end of about two hours he had quite a collection of sightings of the man with the black beard. Seven people had seen him, usually getting into a car. The one thing he was never seen doing was going into the house. He was always coming out.

The man was also seen only at night.

One man, then, who must have seen him, Arimi decided, would be the night watchman at the house across the way.

He crossed the street, entered the front gate and walked around the side of the house to the back. He was dressed, as most schoolboys in Akhana are dressed, in a khaki shirt and shorts, and he was walking barefooted. Anyone seeing him would not observe anything particularly unusual about him except, perhaps, that he was small, though he was twelve years old, and had a rather high, horseshoe-shaped forehead.

He found two women at the back of the house pounding *fufu*. On the ground in front of them was a two-foot-diameter hollowed-out tree trunk which stood at knee height, and the two women, presumably wives or relatives of the steward, held heavy circular poles that would, when standing upright, have reached their shoulders. The poles, being used as pestles, were plunged rhythmically by each woman in turn into the deep hollow in the tree trunk to mash the cassava to the consistency of soft putty.

Without stopping their work or breaking their rhythm, one of the women jerked her chin towards Arimi in a gesture which indicated that she expected to be told what he wanted. From the way she wore her cloth and from the tribal marks cut in her cheeks, Arimi knew that she came from the far north and that she would be unlikely to speak any of the local languages.

"You de getum man for dis place?" he asked.

"Go for market," the woman shouted back.

"Mus' speak wid night watch," Arimi said.

"Go come back nighttime," the woman told him.

"Dassa no good. I de go speak 'um one time. Catchum place night watch go live?"

"Zongo side," the woman said.

"I go give three beni you go take me he house."

The woman shouted something loudly in her own language and a six- or seven-year-old girl in a pink frock came out of a hut behind the woman, who spoke to her in their own language, still without halting the rhythmical pounding of the cassava.

The girl had her hair done up in spiky pigtails, each tied with ribbon which matched her dress. The plaited prickles of hair stuck out all over her head like spines on a sea urchin, and the hair at the root of each spine divided the globe of her scalp into a series of neat squares.

When she had received her orders from her mother, the girl walked towards the gate and then turned and solemnly beckoned Arimi to follow her. As he did so the steady ticktock, ticktock of the pestles in the women's hands continued without a break.

A "zongo" in a West African town is an area set apart for strangers who come from other tribes; the largest population is almost invariably Muslim.

The little girl took him across town and then turned through several streets that were paved with sun-baked mud to the mosque, which looked like a toy constructed out of building blocks. Around the wall of the concrete plinth, which surrounded the building were a number of old men in flowing robes and white skullcaps, sitting cross-legged on the ground. The little girl took Arimi's hand and led him up to one who looked like a most respected old patriarch.

Arimi put his hands together under his chin and bowed to the man, saying, "Salaam Aleikum."

The old man returned the greeting, and then said in the local language, "What do you need, my son?"

"Sir"—Arimi was relieved by the fact that the man spoke a tongue in which they could converse comfortably, but he was a bit overwhelmed by the old man's obvious venerability—"are you the night watch at the gambling man's house?"

"I am."

"Sir, my father, who is big, big man government side and a friend of the President, sent me to ask you if, in the nighttime, you have seen a man with a beard enter or leave the house you guard." If the old man thought the question strange he showed no reaction, but replied simply:

"I have. He comes without the beard, but, I think, carrying it in a bag. Bye and bye he leaves with the beard on his face. Sometimes, a little before the sun comes up, he comes back and he still has the beard. Soon after that he goes away again without the beard. It happens many times on Friday nights. It is a strange game. But if we knew all the reasons for men behaving as they do, our heads would be so full of contradictions that it would buzz like a hive full of angry bees. Is that all you need of me?"

"It is, and I thank you." Arimi bowed again, as he had on his arrival, and repeated, "Salaam Aleikum."

It was close to two o'clock and the sky leaned, with a sodden steamy weight, on everything and everybody.

The inside of the mosque, tiled and empty, looked cool.

Arimi walked past it slowly and continued until he came to a main road and a thick rain tree that stood beside it. In its shade a woman was selling small loaves of corn bread. Arimi bought one and sat down to eat it.

So the man wore a false beard. Mrs. Quarshie's informant had said he was a young man. So—it was simple, Arimi teased himself, all he had to do was to find, in all the tens of thousands of people who lived in Port St. Mary, a young man who occasionally wore a false beard. It would be like trying to identify a mosquito in the cloud of them which rose off the swamps in the evenings.

What else did he know about the man? He used imported perfume and wore a thin gold chain around one wrist.

Arimi chewed his bread, keeping his eyes closed and trying to picture the man he was hunting.

He must have money to hire a taxi once a week for a whole night and to drive close to sixty miles in it. So either he was paid to do what he was doing or he had a lot of money of his own.

What sort of a job would necessitate his spending the whole night with his employer—that is, if he worked for Mrs. Artson-Eskill?

Because he had no answer to that question he opened his eyes.

A bus passed on the street coming from somewhere in the country, sitting askew on its springs because it was so heavily loaded. There were even two boys lying flat amongst the mountain of baggage on the roof carrier.

The corpse of a dog, a casualty of the traffic, was being fought over by some vultures on a small piece of ground nearby. Almost opposite, on the other side of the road, a man was selling newspapers. A magazine called *Sport* had a three-column picture running the full depth of the page. Arimi could just make out the figure of a footballer running towards the camera with both his arms raised above his head in an attitude of triumph. He guessed it would be Tete.

He had finished his bread, so he got up and crossed the road to see if he was correct.

When he got near enough he read the headline beside the picture. It asked: "Will Tete make it 100?" He was just about to pass on when a detail caught his eye. For a moment he felt as if he had been struck by lightning. He squatted in front of the picture, which hung from the front of a packing-case table, to examine it more closely.

Tete was wearing a fine chain, with what looked like a name tag on it, around his left wrist. And, of course, if he had thought of it before, he would have remembered that Tete wore a bracelet. He had read about Tete's attachment to it in a newspaper. It was a good luck charm, a talisman, with a great power of juju attached to it, and Tete had said that he would not go anywhere without it.

Slowly Arimi stood up. It was not a conclusive bit of evidence. Tete was fairly young, and he wore a bracelet. Did he also use perfume and perhaps wear a false beard? If he used a beard, he would probably hide it. But the perfume should be somewhere in his house.

And . . . oh yes . . . perhaps the Fridays when he did not go to Adaja preceded the Saturdays when the Tigers were playing games which required overnight travel.

Now, though the heat was suffocating, Arimi started to run, not at any great speed, but jogging steadily. First he must go to the football park. He had to see the season's fixture list that was nailed up on the board beside the main ticket office.

When he got there queues were already forming, and several people tried to trip him, or cuff him as he made his way to the front, saying:

"I only want to see the fixture list. I don't want to buy a ticket."

The fixture list told exactly the story he wanted it to. The days the bearded man had not engaged the taxi were the same ones that the Tigers had been playing matches which called for overnight travel.

That made the evidence that he was building much stronger, but it was still far from complete.

It was a long way back to Kwadoo's, but Arimi made it in about twenty minutes.

When he got there the taxi driver had gone back on duty. His wife told Arimi, however, that he would be back before sunset to eat and drink. Even when he had enough work to keep him busy from six in the morning to midnight he never failed to come for his evening meal and his African gin. He did not carry the gin with him in the taxi, she explained, because that could get him in trouble with the police, but he always drank at least a half bottle every evening.

Arimi said he would be back in plenty of time to meet Kwadoo, and went home.

There he showered and changed. Mrs. Quarshie was at some women's meeting and Quarshie was still at the hospital, so Arimi told Hassan, the Quarshies' steward, that he would be late for supper, and then dawdled back into town, stopping along the way to price some accessories for his bicycle. He arrived back at Kwadoo's hut well before sunset, and to fill the time went on past King William's castle, which had once been a barracoon in which slaves were held until they could be shipped to the Americas, to the seashore.

From where he stood, at the top of a sandy rise, St. Mary's bay swept out, east and west, in a great curve towards the distant horizon. Behind him, on his left, were the massive walls of the old fortress and on his right Fishermanstown. Over the latter there was a pale grey haze which came from the ovens that were used to smoke the herrings as they were brought in from the fishermen's nets.

The sun was already dipping fast, making silhouettes out of the palm trees along the curve of the bay and striking red-hot splinters off the silky blue and purple surface of the sea.

It was a sight that had a calming effect on Arimi's growing feeling of tension as he thought of what he had planned to do that evening. He was not going to call Kwadoo in to help him because he needed physical backing but because he needed moral support and, perhaps, help at a tactical level. He was quite positive that the man would help him because he recognised in Kwadoo a connection that had something of the flesh in it. It was something akin to affection, and Kwadoo seemed to have for him too.

Perhaps it was love, yet if it was, it was innocent, Arimi being too young and Kwadoo too ignorant to assess their reactions and come up with an answer that would satisfy either a biologist or a behaviourist.

Arimi had been given money by Quarshie at the outset of his mission, and when Kwadoo returned and had finished eating Arimi took him to the market, where he bought him a blue peaked cap and a plastic-covered badge which could be clipped over the breast pocket of a shirt or jacket. Arimi then brought the badge to the public letter writer, took out the white card the badge contained and had him type on it:

Port St. Mary Electricity Board
Representative: Amos Agbeka

"Now," he said, giving the cap and badge to Kwadoo, "you de be important past all. Your name he be Amos Agbeka, and you de work for 'tricity company. Catch sabbee?" Then, switching out of mock pidgin into Kwadoo's tribal language, he said, "Do you know anything about electricity?"

"Mastah, I know small, small," was the reply again in mock pidgin. Then Kwadoo, too, continued in his own language. "One time I worked for a big man as his chauffeur. At the same time I had to do some work in the house, too, and I learned 'tricity."

"Good, then we shall go to a house and you will be the electrician. I will be your small boy. At this house I think there will only be women, because the master and steward will be at the football game. These women speak only *begin* and small pidgin. So we shall get into the house quite easily. After that we must make it seem as if there is trouble with the lights and we have been called by the man who owns the house to fix the trouble. It must also be essential that we check every room."

Kwadoo grinned and said, "Yessah, mastah. Dissee man catch black beard?"

"Sometimes he catchum, sometimes he never catchum."

Kwadoo let out a hoot of laughter and said, "You de number-one hunter, boy." Then shaking his head, he repeated emphatically, "Number one."

However, when he asked where they were going and Arimi told him to Tete's house, he was less enthusiastic.

"How do you know there will be only women there?" he wanted

to know. "This man is a very big man." And in pidgin, "We wrong for dis one, policeman de humbug we too much."

To which Arimi replied, "Any steward for a man like Tete must go to watch him play football when he is playing in Port St. Mary. And if some man is there and he tells us they have no trouble with the 'tricity, then we say, 'We sorry too much someone for office go tell us wrong,' and we go away. So we try, eh, see if I am right?"

Kwadoo shrugged and started the car.

At Tete's house it was as Arimi had foreseen.

Tete's steward was at the football match, and his wife was at home, on guard.

Kwadoo's cap, badge (which of course the woman could not read) and his radiant masculinity—he knew how to trade on the latter—got them inside the house quickly.

However, she took the precaution of staying with them, so Kwadoo went first to the main switch, appeared to be checking it and pulled it out of its connectors just enough to break the feed. Then he went, with Arimi at his heels, to check some of the lights in the house. Of course none of them worked.

In his own language Kwadoo told Arimi, "You go and check the lights upstairs. I will stay here and keep the woman with me." And to her he said, in pidgin, "When I go come you de say you get light for house. Dissee no be true like I show you. You fine, fine woman pass all, but you no sabbee 'tricity. Make you go come here I de show you." He took the cover off one of the light switches and pointed at the connections, beckoning her to come and look. She came shyly, and he got round behind her and proceeded to disconnect the terminals with his arms over her shoulders so that she could not move. He also talked in her ear and stood very close to her, so that his chest was pressed against her shoulders and his loins against the curves of her rump.

Upstairs Arimi quickly looked through drawers and cupboards for any kind of perfume. When he found nothing in either bedroom, he went to the bathroom, and there he found what he was looking for.

He at once returned to the living room and told Kwadoo that all the lights were off upstairs as well but that as soon as Kwadoo was finished with the switch everything would be all right and that they could leave.

Kwadoo reconnected the terminals, slapped the woman's bottom, reset the main switch, turned on one of the lights to show her that it was working and, suppressing his laughter with difficulty, joined Arimi in the taxi.

When they were a safe distance from the house and down on the Marina, beside the sea, Arimi told Kwadoo to pull off the road, under the palm trees, and stop.

It was dark, and Arimi thought of the scene at the football stadium and wondered if it would affect Tete's game if he knew that his house had just been successfully burgled by a small boy and a taxi driver.

As he pulled up Kwadoo said with great excitement in his voice, "You get what you want?"

Arimi put his hand in his pocket and pulled out a bottle of aftershave lotion and, dabbing a little on the back of his hand, offered it to Kwadoo to smell.

The taxi driver took the boy's hand with a curious gentleness, lifted it to his face and sniffed noisily.

Then with his eyes wide open he told Arimi, "Dissee be de one, de same, same one. You clever pass all, boy. Way de be clever pass all."

Arimi said, "It is good, but it is not all. It is only the beginning. Now we must go back to my house and I must tell my father everything."

When he got home Mrs. Quarshie was inclined to scold him for staying out so long, but Arimi anticipated her.

"I came home to tell you what I was doing," he explained, "but you were out." To Quarshie he said, "You told me, sir, to find the man. I think I did." And gave an account of the activities that had kept him out so late.

Quarshie squeezed the boy's shoulder and said, "It was very well done, and it means now that we must do more. I do not have to go back to the hospital until about eleven o'clock, so how would it be if, after all, I took you to see Tete? None of the evidence we have tells us anything yet except, perhaps, that Tete visits Mrs. A.E. If he does, then it means that he will know Grace, and perhaps, just perhaps, we can frighten him into talking about her."

"Why would you be able to frighten him, Quarshie?" Mrs. Quarshie asked.

"Because we have made our way onto secret ground and where there are secrets there must be things to hide. Very few people can hide things without getting nervous."

"Why hide things about someone who has gone missing?"

"I don't know, and I won't even speculate about it until I have talked to the man," Quarshie replied cautiously.

CHAPTER FIVE

"Soft lips often hide sharp teeth."

The radio sports commentator said, "Tete never played better. It was as if the devil, Okolebamidele, was driving him. As if he had to prove again to himself what everyone else knows . . . that he is the greatest. I was sorry for his opponents. Even when they played well he made their efforts look like schoolboy football. Over and over again he had the defence moving the wrong way. The goalkeeper, whom he beat three times, said to me afterwards, 'It was like facing a demon.' "

Quarshie turned off the car radio. He said, "That's not the way athletes usually break records. They move in on them with care and caution. What devil was driving him, do you suppose?"

Mrs. Quarshie had been called out to attend one of her patients who was in labour, and Quarshie and Arimi were on their way to visit Tete without her.

As they turned a corner the lights of the car showed them a small boy climbing a tree to steal a pawpaw.

Arimi was tired. It had been a long day but he, felt, the greatest moment was yet to come.

Quarshie had rung Tete earlier and told him that he wanted to visit him to congratulate him, and also to discuss something important.

Mrs. Quarshie had asked how Tete had reacted to Quarshie's request.

"He sounded as if he was just waking up. First he was confused, then I think he connected my name with Grand Banane when he was so ill and I attended him. It was like someone who had been groping around in the dark and has suddenly found a light switch. It's extraordinary that telephone wires can carry human feelings so accurately. He needs to see me, I think, because, as once before when he was in trouble, I happened to be the one who could help him."

"He's in trouble?"

Quarshie had nodded. "He thinks he is," he had replied, and then paused before adding, "And I think he is."

Arimi, remembering that statement now, asked, "Why do you think he is in trouble, sir?"

Quarshie frowned, staring straight ahead down the beam of the headlights, and shook his head. "I don't know. The game of football he played and the tone of his voice when he spoke to me. The way he appears to have played this game was almost as if it was an act of desperation. And then he was so disorientated on the phone. What I thought I heard was a cry for help."

Quarshie braked the car to a stop in front of the house and they got out. There was a policeman on duty outside the gate. He saluted Quarshie and said:

"The man de for inside tell me make I go say you to go knock on de door, sah."

And as Quarshie moved to comply, followed by Arimi, the guard added. "He never go say nothing 'bout piccin."

Quarshie smiled and told the policeman, "The piccin, Officer, de belong to me, my son."

"Yes, sah." The man stood aside, smiling hugely. "Dat good, sah. Big lion get small lion. Very good, sah."

At the door Tete's steward said, "Please, sah, make you de come inside. Mastah he dey for dissee room, maybe small sick. Play football like he fit kill hisself. After . . . he send everybody for he own house. Stay by hisself. Now no go eat chop at all, at all."

Inside the room they found Tete standing with his back to them, aimlessly looking at a framed photograph of himself scoring a goal. He was tall and slender up to his shoulders, which were spread across his torso like the head of a T-square.

When he turned to greet them he stared with frozen-faced intensity at Quarshie. Without changing his expression he held out his hand and said, "Hullo, Doctor."

"Hullo, man," Quarshie replied. "I'm surprised to find you alone on a big day like this. This is my son, Arimi. He's a great admirer of yours."

Tete shook his head. "Nobody should admire me," he said, "nobody."

"Oh, but you are the best footballer this country has ever seen. You proved it again tonight."

Tete was not listening; he was staring at Arimi. "What do you want?" he asked. "My autograph? My picture? Here." He snatched a handful of signed pictures and pushed them towards Arimi. "Here. Take them, and if you have any savvy you will burn them."

Quarshie said quietly, "Take them, boy, and go and wait for me in the car." Arimi glanced wide-eyed at Quarshie and then did as he was told.

After he had left the room Tete said, "He's very intelligent. How are you, Doctor? I think I'm sick."

Quarshie frowned and asked, "Do you have any beer?"

"Of course. Justice," Tete shouted for his steward. "Get beer for mastah, one time. Sit down, Doctor, sit down."

When the steward returned with the beer Quarshie said, "Get beer for your mastah, too."

Tete said, "I don't drink it."

"You never drink it?"

"I'm in training."

"And at this moment I have appointed myself your doctor. So put yourself into my hands and do as I tell you. Justice, fetch master some beer." As the steward left the room Quarshie told Tete, "Take off your clothes and lie down on the couch. I want to examine you."

The footballer obeyed as if Quarshie's orders had bereft him of his will. Quarshie's hands were not only large, they were gentle, and he handled his patient in the same way that he handled his sculpture, working along the tense muscles until they were tense no more, with confidence and a kind of compassion that had the beginning of the desired effect on Tete.

When the beer came Quarshie poured some and gave it to him, saying, "This is medicine. Drink it." And when the glass was empty he filled it, gave it to the footballer again and watched him swallow its contents for a second time.

After that he told Tete, "I'm going to work over every muscle in your body and I want you to cooperate by letting go, relaxing each one as I come to it. I am going to start with your feet. Later we shall talk. And while I work on you I don't want you to think of me as a masseur. I am a friend who is privileged to be able to get this close to you to retune this perfect instrument, your body, and get all its elements in balance again. You really tore them apart with that game you played this evening."

Tete's fixed expression was beginning to melt. He closed his eyes and gave in self-indulgently to Quarshie's attention.

While he worked Quarshie watched himself a little uneasily. He was deliberately taking advantage of his patient's defencelessness to penetrate the man's confidence because he knew that his treatment would be felt emotionally as well as physically.

Eventually he said, "Now, how do you feel?"

It was as if Tete awoke from a sleep for the second time that evening at the sound of Quarshie's voice. He turned slowly on his back and blinked up at the Doctor. "I feel quite different," he said.

"Good. Having done with the first aid, we now have to tackle the fundamental cause of your problem. O.K.?"

Evasively Tete replied, "But I feel all right. I was a bit tense. I am all right now, thank you. I don't think there is anything else to talk about."

Quarshie decided not to waste time cajoling the information he wanted out of Tete. He realized that the most effective way of dealing with the situation now was to hit him and hit him hard.

The Doctor sat down and in a quiet conversational tone of voice said, "You mean to tell me that the case of traumatic shock I have been treating has nothing to do with your visits to Mrs. Artson-Eskill? Or that false beard you wear? Or the fact that her daughter is missing?"

Tete lay still, and Quarshie could almost see the rigidities that he had just massaged away creeping back into the footballer's muscles.

"You are going to have to talk about these things or continue to go through that same kind of anxiety."

Tete found his voice. "How do you know about those things?" he asked. "Who has been talking to you? That fat bitch?"

"Mrs. A.E., if that is who you mean, came and told me that Grace was missing. She asked me to see if I could find her. She did not tell me anything about you. What is your relationship with her?"

Tete ignored the question. "Have you found Grace?" He was sitting up.

"Do you think I could?"

"I don't understand you."

"When did you last see her?"

"About a week ago."

"It's important." Quarshie spoke very deliberately. "When exactly did you last see her?"

"Two Fridays ago."

"At her mother's."

"Yes."

"When you went from the 'fat bitch's' bed to hers?"

"Yes." Quarshie could hardly hear the word. "What are you, a magician of some sort?"

"Once one knows that a personable and handsome young athlete is visiting a fat middle-aged woman's house late at night and at regular intervals, it is not too difficult to figure what purpose his visits serve. As for the girl . . . she is missing, and you are showing many of the symptoms of nervous shock. So the odds would be in favour of your condition being due to something that may have happened to her."

Tete did not reply.

Quarshie decided to hit him again.

"Were both women paying for your services, or only the mother?"

Tete was off the couch and had thrown himself at Quarshie as swiftly, blindly and instinctively as he had scored his three goals earlier in the evening, though with less skill.

As his hands reached for Quarshie's throat, the Doctor brought his right fist up into Tete's extended solar plexus and the footballer collapsed with a retching sound, hugging his knees.

Quarshie let him lie on the floor to recover his breath without touching him. Then, when Tete sat up again, Quarshie put his hand gently on his shoulder and said, "I am not condemning you for your behaviour. Your gesture of giving my son a handful of pictures told me you had gone to extremes of self-condemnation already. I am only asking questions to which I have to have the answers if I am to have any hope of finding Grace. So I want your help and not your antagonism. Do you understand?"

Tete nodded his head slowly and said, "I'm sorry." Quarshie squeezed his shoulder gently to acknowledge the apology, then sat back in his chair.

"All right. Let's start again, this time at the beginning. Tell me what you know—not what you feel, but what you know—about Grace."

Tete turned and sat on the floor facing Quarshie. He had his knees drawn up and his elbows on them, with his hands clasped in front of him. His skin was a light copper colour, with shades of a darker brown where the muscles sloped down into the valleys between them.

"Perhaps we should begin with your association with Mrs. A.E. When did it start?"

"She defended me in a breach-of-contract case."

"And won?"

"Yes."

"And?"

"She did not want any money for it."

"She wanted you?"

"Yes. It seemed an easy way to settle the debt. But it was only the beginning. It turned to blackmail."

"How?"

"She led me to commit perjury during the trial, then held the threat of revealing the fact over my head."

"I see."

"And she uses it like a whip. Bitch."

"And the girl?"

Tete shook his head. "I think I know what you mean. No. She is careful of people. I mean, her mother doesn't care if people get hurt so long as she gets what she wants. Grace . . ." He dropped his head and sat staring at the floor between his feet. Presently, without raising his head, he continued, "She is the first woman who ever tried to find in me more than anyone can see of me on the outside, more than the athletic sex thing, you know?" He looked up. "Grace had a close friendship with another man before she knew me who taught her a lot. He was a West Indian she knew in Paris."

"I didn't know she went to France."

"From England. Perhaps she met him in London. He was a poet. A Haitian. She talks of him frequently. She has often told me that he made her into a different person. She is trying to do the same thing to me."

Quarshie noted that they were talking of Grace in the present tense, and it reinforced his feeling that the footballer was a spectator in what had happened to Grace and was only peripherally involved.

"Would you call Grace an intellectual?"

"I don't really know what that means. She knows a lot more than people like myself and the people of the village where she lives."

"She does not have much to do with them."

"Because they don't need her. If they needed her she would do anything for them, I am sure. She says that they are quite convinced that the ancestors and the gods know what is right and wrong. That they have all the answers to the problems of a world in which aeroplanes, cars, electricity and science are changing everything. When they believe things like that, she told me, you can't expect them to listen to her."

Quarshie began to alter his initial opinion of Grace.

"But she means a lot to you?" he asked.

"More than I ever believed a woman could. My mother had eleven children. With her I was just one of many."

Quarshie checked off in his mind what he knew now and what else he needed to know. Finding a gap, he enquired:

"Does she ever talk about her father?"

"Not much. He was a professor at the University. I think he died when she was in primary school. She said, once, that he used to spoil her."

"What happened to the Haitian boyfriend?"

"She went with him to Port au Prince and he was jailed by the Tonton Macoute. Later they killed him. After that she came back here."

"And her relationship with her mother?"

"Is terrible. She hates her."

"Why?"

"Because she is . . . she calls her an 'elitist,' a crooked elitist."

"So why does she stay with her?"

"She wants to become a writer and write about Africa, but she cannot do that unless she lives here. She is planning to move away but her mother won't give her any money, so she is looking for work."

"On that Friday night, when you last saw her, did she say anything about leaving?"

"Not that I remember."

"Yet you are very upset because she has gone. Surely you must suspect something."

Tete got up off the floor and went and poured himself more beer. Then he went to the door, called his steward and told him to bring more beer for Quarshie and to bring sandwiches.

After he had settled himself again on the floor at Quarshie's feet he said, "She told me she had been visiting a place called Murder Mountain. Do you know it?"

"I have heard of it. Isn't it in Choboland somewhere?"

"It's one of the peaks on their hills. It is the place where in the old days murderers were executed by a priest. There is a lot of bad juju about the place."

"Did she go there by herself?"

"No."

"So who were her companions?"

"She wouldn't tell me."

"Did she say why she was going?"

"Her father was an anthropologist, and she said that what she was doing would have interested him. She said it was something I would not understand. But I know about Murder Mountain and Rat Cave, where they put the murderers' bodies after they were dead. She shouldn't be going there."

"Yet you didn't stop her because she feels superior and won't listen to you?"

"She is superior to me."

Quarshie said, "Soft lips often hide sharp teeth. You make judgements too easily, perhaps. Particularly of yourself. I must go because I have work to do at the hospital. If you remember anything else that will help me to find Grace, contact me at once."

As Quarshie rose Tete got up with him, and as they approached the door together the steward came in with the sandwiches.

"Eat, my friend," Quarshie told the footballer, "and don't allow yourself to get too depressed. I may need you to help me, and you won't be any use if you are only partly in command of your emotions."

When Quarshie opened the car door Arimi was fast asleep, and the Doctor did not disturb him. He woke up when Quarshie started the engine, and in a sleepy voice he asked, "Did he tell you anything important, sir?"

Quarshie sighed and said, "Not as much as I might have hoped. But, yes, I suppose he told me quite a lot that will be useful to us."

Arimi heard what the Doctor said in a fuddled sort of way, but he heard the "us" quite clearly, and contentedly allowed himself to drift off to sleep again.

CHAPTER SIX

*"On a twig in the forest the butterfly looks
beautiful. In the mouth of a lizard it is
just another meal."*

Mrs. Quarshie's patient kept her until 3 A.M., and since Quarshie's work had kept him out late as well they did not meet again until they sat down together to eat a late breakfast. When they had night calls they slept in separate rooms so as not to disturb each other.

First Mrs. Quarshie asked about her husband's work at the hospital and learned that strict isolation procedures were in force and that Quarshie was acting only in an advisory capacity and had had no contact with the patient suffering from lasser fever.

And her delivery? It had caused her anxiety, Mrs. Quarshie admitted. The woman had had a cesarean section for a previous delivery, and Mrs. Quarshie had had the operating theatre and a doctor standing by to repeat the process if there had been complications. The woman was the wife of a tribal chief, and he had insisted on a natural delivery to satisfy some traditional law. Men! Mrs. Quarshie had almost bitten the word out of her mouth. They were prepared to sacrifice their wives to satisfy some idiotic belief that came to them from their equally ignorant fathers. Fortunately there had been no complications. Afterwards, however, the Chief had accused her, Mrs. Quarshie, of having been bought by white men for suggesting that another cesarean would be safer.

Quarshie enjoyed his wife's indignation as much as any of her other characteristics. She would, he knew, challenge and fight the devil himself if she felt he was responsible for some kind of idiocy, and it would be a no-holds-barred contest. Yet, when she was in his arms, she was more pliant and yielding than the clay his mother had used to make cooking pots.

"And Tete?" Mrs. Quarshie asked.

Quarshie told her of their meeting.

"Then you don't think he is involved in her disappearance?" she said when he had finished.

"I don't know. If he is I don't think he knows it. Someone might be using him. I think she is really too important to him for him to think of hurting her in any way."

"So what are you going to do, now?"

"I must talk to Mrs. A.E. again. Without any concrete clues to guide us the only way to make any progress is to work on the people who knew the girl. Apart from Tete, Mrs. A.E. and the man the Tonton Macoute murdered she does not appear to have any other friends, but Mrs. A.E. must know of others, if they exist."

To Quarshie's surprise, Mrs. Artson-Eskill had been quite willing to see him. She asked him to meet her at the leper colony, some ten miles outside Port St. Mary; she had said that she felt that they shouldn't be seen together. She had reason, she told him, to visit the leper colony around noon, and no one would think it unnatural if he, a doctor, also happened to be there at the same time.

It was a place that Quarshie had known quite well when, as a young pathologist, he had taken an interest in developing a series of tests to determine the effectiveness of certain new drugs on the thickening of the nerve trunks in anaesthetic leprosy.

So the colony was familiar, and it never failed to depress him because of the feeling of malignant blight that affected the place despite everyone's efforts to brighten it.

The "hospital" had dated back to the colonial days, and it had come into being in a haphazard way. A few acres of land beside the sea had been provided by the government, and small grants of money had been made to the lepers and their families to build themselves mud-walled huts roofed with corrugated iron. A one-room clinic, which was visited once a week by medical staff from Port St. Mary, was also erected. Otherwise the patients had been left to organise themselves, so it had grown up much like any ordinary African village.

With these images in his memory Quarshie was quite astonished, when he turned his car into the entrance, to find the amount of change that had taken place.

What was most evident was that money had been spent carefully and sensibly. Land had been broken for cultivation; there was a shop, an office for the supervisor, and concrete pathways had been laid so that those suffering with infected feet need not walk through the dust and the mud.

Quarshie was early, and it was the supervisor who explained that Mrs. Artson-Eskill had been the motivating force behind the changes that had taken place. She was the Chairman of the Board of the Leprosy Society, and she had not only determined the priorities for the changes that had been accomplished but she had wide-reaching plans for the future. In fact, the man assured Quarshie, he knew that she financed many of them out of her own pocket, though nothing was ever said about it. Officially it was always money from the Society that was used, but he, who was himself a leper, was the treasurer, and so he knew that there had not been enough money in the fund to pay for everything. The lepers, too, were paid for their work, but the only person who ever handled any money on their paydays was Mrs. Artson-Eskill.

"The people love her," the superintendent told Quarshie, "and treat her as if she was their queen."

When she arrived, almost an hour late, that statement was proved to be correct, for her progress, as she walked around with Quarshie and talked to the patients, was truly regal.

Afterwards Mrs. Artson-Eskill had the girl who accompanied her carry some folding chairs down to the beach and put them under a palm-thatched shelter. The girl, Quarshie assumed, would be a product of Mrs. Artson-Eskill's extended family, a cousin perhaps, who was serving a term of more or less indentured slavery. No one in an extended family ever went without essential support if one relative could provide it, but any help could easily foster the feeling that dutiful benevolence calls for a dutifully menial response.

Quarshie knew that the child, who was about twelve years old, would be at Mrs. Artson-Eskill's beck and call to carry out what might often be demeaning tasks.

Seated, the lady looked like two great lumps of baker's dough topped by the almost spherical blob of her head partly tied up in a silk head-tie with its two broad, flamboyant antennae.

Mrs. Artson-Eskill did not allow Quarshie, once they were seated, to open his mouth, despite the fact that it was he who had called for the meeting. She expected to be attacked, and she knew from her courtroom experience that the best defence was to take the initiative.

"So you've already arrived at the point, Doctor, where you have discovered that the only evidence you can get will be from me. No, don't deny it. I have thought a lot about this thing, and I am sure that I have some of the information you need, though I may be sitting too close to it to see it clearly. However, I have prepared some thoughts for you which may help the investigation." She looked sideways out of her heavy-lidded eyes. "I will be as honest with you as I can be and still preserve my self-respect. First, let's take a look at one of the skeletons in the family cupboard. My late husband and Grace's father, Mister Artson-Eskill. He married me under false pretences. I thought he wanted me—he didn't. He wanted my money and the access I could give him to prominent people.

"There are those who might think it odd that I would need a man. But, as you must know, even the skinniest of us need masculine attention, Doctor. Suppose you give that want, that need in a skinny woman the algebraic symbol x, then my need, since I have ten times the amount of flesh to be satisfied, would be a factor of 10 x. Do you understand what I am saying?

"So, Artson-Eskill was a fraud. He used the money I gave him for his anthropological research and to travel. It wasn't difficult for him to make a name for himself because African anthropologists are few and far between. And of course he made a fool of Grace by filling her head full of romantic nonsense about the past. I wanted her to take law: that's where the money and the power lie. You were in Canada, weren't you? While you were there did you ever count the number of people in top positions in politics and in industry who have a legal background? And if you want to help people—like the men and women in the leprosarium, for instance—then you have to have money and power, and lots of both.

"But Grace will not have it that way. Power, according to her, must come out of the people, out of their unity and desire to work for the common good, which is just plain nonsense. If you put a variety of animals in a cage together and watch them to see which one will survive, you will see it is the lion—or rather the lioness, because she has the strength, the cunning and the motivation. She has to breed and raise young lions."

"The law of the jungle," Quarshie said softly.

"And what is wrong with that? Survival is what the world is all about. It's no good being full of romantic ideas if you don't survive.

"Anyway, Grace has balked for years at everything I suggest. She is going to be like her father, who was prepared to let other people do the dirty work and then live happily off the proceeds of their realism and industry. My people have a saying, 'On a twig in the forest the butterfly looks beautiful. In the mouth of a lizard it is just another meal.'

"Now does that answer one of the questions you asked the other day? I gave you an evasive answer, then, about my relationship with Grace. I have only one thing to add: she is my daughter, my flesh and blood, a part of me like my hand or my foot, so of course, I am not inclined to expose her to injury if I can help it because I shall only be hurting myself. Does that tell you what you want to know?"

Quarshie said, "It is useful information. I do, however, have another important question. Through sources I cannot name—"

"Oh, no you don't," Mrs. Artson-Eskill snapped at him. "I am paying you. What my money buys for you belongs to me as well."

"Your money does not buy anything for me," Quarshie told her bluntly. "We have been over this ground before. The information came to me without the passage of any money, yours or mine, and if you are going to take that attitude I am not going to continue any further with the case."

Mrs. Artson-Eskill gave Quarshie the same sidelong glance she had given him before and said, "How quickly you get petulant. I was only testing you to see how reliable you would be with off-the-record information. So these sources you cannot name have given you information that has led to a question you want to ask me. What is it?"

Quarshie watched the waves curl in onto the sandy beach which stretched away into the distance as far as he could see. There was a thunderhead out on the horizon, but between it and the shoreline the sky was blue. Beside them along the beach the palm trees leaned negligently against the wind, and Quarshie thought of the African belief that they were the strongest of all trees because, so long as they were properly rooted, no wind, however fierce, could ever break their stems. They "rolled with the punches," as his boxing instructor in Canada had phrased it. And he would roll with the punches now, because more and more he was coming to believe that Grace needed help.

He said, "Yes. I have learned that your daughter was getting involved in some kind of anthropological or archeological work in the Choboland area. Do you know who might take her on that kind of expedition?"

Mrs. Artson-Eskill stared at the sea with a louring intensity that matched that of the thundercloud on the horizon.

When she spoke Quarshie had to lean forward to hear what she was saying.

"History is repeating itself," she muttered, "another anthropologist who thinks he is on to a good thing. Wilson-Sarkey. Yes, even down to the double-barrelled name. He is a lecturer at the University. He's over forty, married and has two children. At least Artson-Eskill was my age and single." Suddenly she turned to Quarshie and blazed at him, "Why am I haunted by these people who spend their lives digging into the past? What business is it of theirs how our ancestors lived? Why can't they let them be?" Then all at once she seemed to deflate, actually to grow a little smaller, and in a quieter tone of voice she said, "Grace has been seeing this man for some time. I have never met him." She looked tired. "I must go back to the office. Help me up, Doctor." Once on her feet, she called, "Rosebud. Rosebud! Isn't that a ridiculous name for an African girl? Whoever saw a black rosebud? Please tell the girl, when she comes, to take the chairs to the car. I must go and have a word with the superintendent before I leave. These people here are the only ones who have any gratitude for what one does for them." And she heaved her body slowly up the slope of the sand, to be followed a few minutes later by Rosebud, carrying the chairs, and Quarshie, who had a curious feeling that he was, in fact, attending someone—a kind of female Nero, perhaps—who was genetically disposed to wear the purple.

When he got back to his house he found Mrs. Quarshie in a bad mood because the washerman had scorched one of her white overalls with the electric iron.

"I have told him a million times not to use it with the heat control turned right up. I have only worn that thing twice. The man is an idiot."

She was behaving as imperiously as Mrs. Artson-Eskill, Quarshie thought.

The "man" had probably only left his bush village a few months, or at the most, a year or two ago, so electrical gadgetry would be as strange to him as flying an aeroplane might be to Mrs. Quarshie.

"And?" his wife demanded of him. "What did you get out of her?"

"That she likes to order people about. And when they don't measure up to what she expects of them, she gets very scornful."

Mrs. Quarshie looked up at her husband with a frown and then, making the connection he intended, said, "Well, Issaker really is a fool, isn't he?"

Quarshie told her gently, "But a very faithful one. He would die for you if you told him to. So Issaker will be twice as upset because you are angry with him."

"Poor Issaker. I will make him happy again in just a little while. But he has to learn, Quarshie; he has to learn. And now what about that woman?"

Quarshie sighed. "I don't know," he said. "In a way I would like to believe there is no good in her at all. But actually she is pathetic. And terribly confused. She has so much and she has no idea of how to handle it. Royal blood, lots of money, social position, a thriving law practice, a sharp mind . . . and great unhappiness. She does good work for the lepers—they are 'her people,' 'her' subjects, and their gratitude makes her feel benevolent. I am afraid that's the reason she is so charitable . . . Oh," he interrupted himself, "I found her such an absorbing study that I have forgotten to tell you the most important thing. When you are free we are going to visit a professor of anthropology at the University. He was one, perhaps the only one, of Grace's boyfriends. Mrs. A.E. does not approve of him at all."

"Then I probably shall," Mrs. Quarshie said emphatically.

. . . *and it occasions appalling terror because it is a diabolical force for evil. In our mouths it has the sound "borigi," or "killer breath" . . .*

CHAPTER SEVEN

*"Like a hedgehog with poison on
every prickle."*

Mrs. Quarshie said indignantly, "The money they spent on this place!"

She and Quarshie were driving up a long avenue of royal palms on the campus of the University of Akhana. Quarshie had attended the institution, which lay a little way outside the town, when it had been a humble college associated with the University of London and less than a quarter of its present size.

He said, "A lot of people point to its extravagance, but you know, I think the money that was put into it was well spent. The British left us nothing to be proud of in the way of architecture. And the people of a young nation need something to look at and remember and say, when they visit other countries, 'Ours is better than theirs.' The one thing the British did leave us was the practice of creating ornamental gardens, and that is something which has been used here and even, perhaps, improved upon."

The University occupied the crest and flanks of a small hill, and the architect had adopted the architecture from the Moors. The Moorish designs, besides being graceful, were supremely functional for a country in which intense heat is a commonplace. The architect, curiously, was an Italian, and in giving Akhana its most impressive buildings he had modernised—that is, simplified—his model.

The gardeners, of course, could not go wrong. For the surroundings they used the English concept of wide acres of parkland and then planted them with trees and shrubs which produced a shimmering brilliance of colour that could compete favourably with the best in stained-glass windows. Besides the imperial dignity of the royal palms the campus abounded in flamboyants (sometimes called flame trees), jacarandas, tulip trees, frangipanis and bushes of hibiscus, multicoloured bougainvillea, jasmine, pulmbago and great beds of scarlet and yellow canna lilies. Besides the flowering trees there were pink mahogany trees that could, when fully grown, reach a hundred and sixty feet in height, West African ebony that could climb to close to a hundred feet, sapele mahogany and silk cotton trees that might, one day, stretch up towards the clouds for almost two hundred feet.

Mrs. Quarshie said, "Are surroundings more important than people's health? The money spent here could have provided the country with, I don't know, perhaps hundreds of clinics or at least half a dozen good hospitals."

Quarshie pulled the car into the shade of an akee apple tree. As he switched off the engine he replied, "The kind of argument you could start on that subject could be classified in the 'Which came first, the chicken or the egg?' category."

He stretched and added, "Now, the good professor sounded amiable enough when I spoke with him on the phone, so let's hope nothing has happened to upset him since then."

They entered a hallway that stood two stories high and had a vaulted ceiling. The corridors which led off it were spacious, and the tall windows were shaded with fretted shutters. Entering the building from the suffocating heat outside was an act of refreshment.

Professor Wilson-Sarkey's office, on the second floor, was a section of a much bigger room that was divided into smaller areas by tall movable jalousied screens, and as in the hallway, there was a breeze that was here aided by electric fans.

The professor was a small, neat man, with quick squirrel-like movements and a squirrel-like alertness in his glance. The only oddity about his appearance was the way he wore his hair. Afro hairstyles were rare on the campus, even amongst the students, and amongst the staff they were virtually taboo. The professor, however, had invented a style which was part Afro, part something which was distinctly his own: his hair was cut so that he appeared to be wearing it on the back of his head like a streamlined faring to the truly massive frontal segment of his skull.

He got up as they came in and fussed around them as he got them seated, saying, "But this is a pleasure. Two of the people I have most wanted to meet for a long time. Mrs. Quarshie, please settle yourself here. I am sure you will find this chair quite comfortable. And you, Doctor, over her. Now,"—he went back to his own chair—"you have chosen a good day for a visit. None of this stuff on my desk is urgent and I have an easy day on tutorials, so I am completely at your disposal. Other days, of course, I don't allow people to disturb my attention to my pupils. So often the flame of their interest is small and blows out so easily if one does not nourish it carefully. You are one of the distinguished alumni of this place, aren't you, Doctor? How does it feel to come back? And why have you come? I mean, why are you here to see me?"

He put his fingertips together and looked from one of them to the other with a manner he had obviously developed to indicate to his students that he surrendered the floor to them.

Quarshie approached his subject obliquely.

"Anthropology and archeology must be fascinating. Do you find, Professor, that your work leads to any sort of connection with things that are going on today?"

"Oh, indeed yes. Why, just last night I was talking to a colleague from America who was impressed with a discovery he had made in the Dagussi area, a region that has been touched only lightly by white men's cultures. He found that, in the morning, farmers would leave their produce beside the track, indicating the price they wanted for it by the number of small red stones in front of it. A purchaser would then take what he needed and leave the correct price beside the red stones, Later the farmer would collect the money that had laid there probably for hours. You know of this custom, of course, but our American friend did not. He was, as I said, most impressed, and I was able to tell him that it was a very old tradition related to one our people used to call silent barter. In the Chobo area, for instance, the farmers used to put their produce, oh, generations ago, at a well-known spot near a certain tree. Then, when other traders found that what had been put out was sufficient to warrant a deal, they would replace the produce with, perhaps, tools, or other items the farmers needed. They would then take the yams or whatever they had traded for and leave what they considered to be a fair price in their own goods. The whole transaction was, you see, carried out without either party seeing the other. It was obviously an era when trust was more highly regarded than it became after the Europeans arrived. But surely you did not come to discuss that kind of thing with me."

"There is a slight connection," Quarshie replied, "through your interest and knowledge of Choboland. You have, I believe, an apprentice assistant named Grace Artson-Eskill?" He was watching the professor very closely, and he thought he saw a faint shadow of a recoil.

"Oh, but indeed I do. Most charming and intelligent young lady. If only there were a few more like her around. I have great expectations for her: I am hoping I can bring her back into the academic fold. Why are you interested in her, may I ask?"

"Her mother reports that she has disappeared."

"I am afraid I don't understand."

"She has not been home for more than a week."

"Ah, young people do take it into their heads sometimes to go off without telling anyone. She will turn up. Is there perhaps a man?"

"Do you say that because she might have mentioned anyone to you?"

"She did."

"Did she say anything about him?"

"We did not discuss the matter." The professor made it sound as if the subject was a distasteful one.

Quarshie thought he had touched a painful spot, and moved away from it. Pressure there would put the man on the defensive. At the right moment he could prod the place again when the man was off his guard, and it might startle him into an unconsidered reaction. To change the subject he asked:

"Did you know Grace's father?"

"Of course. A rare man, an authentic scholar. He laid the ground rules that I and my colleagues follow today."

"Did you see anything of him in his daughter?"

"Oh, certainly. The greatest force in Artson-Eskill's life was scientific curiosity. He never felt that he had come to final solutions to any piece of research. He once told me that the more questions that were left to be answered, the better the job he felt he had done. Grace is full of the same kind of curiosity."

"And his wife?"

"What about her?"

"Did you know her?"

The professor considered his answer and then said, very deliberately, "I chose not to. And that is all I need to, or intend to, say on that subject."

"Would you be surprised if I told you that I find her curiously defenceless?"

"Like a hedgehog with poison on every prickle. No, Doctor, I would rather not talk about her."

"All right. Let's go back to Grace. Can you think of anything she said that might have indicated that she was going away anywhere?"

"My dear Doctor Quarshie, I am surprised that you are spending time and energy on this, this trivial matter. The newspapers and the stories that are told in the markets indicate that you are a man who usually gives his time only to hunting those who assassinate presidents, commit murders that can harm the international image of our country, involve incipient coups or the exploitation of our people by unsavoury foreign agents. Now, here you are trying to find a young woman who has run away from home. It's so out of character. Don't you agree?"

Quarshie shook his head slowly. "No, I don't. I once read a paper about Africans which called our people "The Feeling Society." It suggested that because our sensibilities had not been as blunted by steel, chromium, plastic and concrete, the natural barriers Westerners have placed between themselves and the rest of the world, we had retained a sensitivity to each other and our surroundings which the others have lost. I believe there is some truth in that. I have a capability to feel vibrations that are of a higher frequency than quite a lot of other people. The vibrations in relation to Grace's disappearance are bad—even frightening. So I do not regard it as a 'trivial matter,' Professor. I would wager my medical degree on the instinct I have that tells me there is something rotten going on. You might say that I can smell it. That's why I am anxious to learn from you all you can tell me."

Again Quarshie sensed that the pulse of the man who sat opposite to him became, momentarily, a little fainter.

Then the professor shook his head with a smile and said, "So much for scientific and academic discipline, eh, Doctor? You are resorting to a species of necromancy and divination. I am, in fact, surprised that you have not said that you have been in contact with your ancestors."

And he leaned forward, adding in a tone of voice that became flat and almost ugly, "Doctor, I refuse to gossip about my friends. Grace had a boyfriend. There is nothing unusual in that. Who he is or what he does is none of my business. Now, I have to prepare for a tutorial that is due to start in ten minutes. Don't take my asperity of a few moments ago too seriously. I really do hope that you are successful in finding the young woman, and if you find some specific evidence which suggests that I might be able to help you, please call on me again. It is not often I have the privilege of entertaining beautiful women and distinguished men in this home of science, logic and academic study." He stressed the last five words so that they sounded like a rebuke.

Neither Quarshie nor his wife spoke until they were sitting in their car.

Then, before he switched on the ignition, Quarshie said with a trace of a smile, "Would you consider that the prognosis might be that he is a little more sensitive in this matter than he should be and that there is perhaps a valid reason for us to probe a little deeper?"

"Absolutely, Doctor," Mrs. Quarshie replied. "The patient should be kept under strict observation." After a pause she added seriously, "He gives me a creepy feeling. We had a master like him at school. He always pretended to like us. But he didn't, he hated us. So when he caught us doing anything wrong he doubled the punishment. He was a horrid man."

CHAPTER EIGHT

*"A man who is born to be hanged will never
be drowned."*

Only those nearing senility in Port St. Mary ever thought of the city
the way "it used to be." Most of the others had grown up while the
bulk of the changes were taking place, so they had become accus-
tomed to the continuous destruction of the shape of the immediate
past. This often occurred before what was being destroyed had
served an even modestly useful life. They had also got used to a
constant upsurge of new forms which were frequently graceless,
crude and lacking in that comfortable feeling that buildings and
clothes have after they have been well used.

As Mrs. Quarshie drove north along Independence Avenue she
saw, but did not consider, the high-rise office blocks on each side of
the road. She saw but gave no thought to the supermarkets, the
discos, the boutiques, the filling stations and all the rest of the
debris and paraphernalia of the twentieth-century city. So she did
not recognise the contradictions that derived from the fact that the
people had changed in their behaviour and appearance very little
indeed from those who had inhabited the city fifty years earlier. To
anyone who took the trouble to examine them more closely it would
also have become apparent that many of the people had changed
even less in the way they thought and in their beliefs.

Mrs. Quarshie, however, was not interested in the phenomenon
of change. She was concentrating, rather tensely, on her driving,
and worrying about the experience which lay ahead of her.

She had not told Quarshie, when he suggested that she renew her
acquaintance with Asteteompong, that she was not sure that she
could handle the man because that, she felt, would have been to
Quarshie a surprising admission of weakness. She knew that her

husband did not set her on a pedestal, but she also knew that his expectations of her were very high.

Her trip north followed a discussion, which had included Arimi, of Grace's disappearance. It had taken place the previous evening, after Mrs. Quarshie and the Doctor had returned from their visit to Professor Wilson-Sarkey. It had been Quarshie's opinion that none of the people with whom they had talked had been frank and that there was more to be learned from each of them before they widened the net to bring in any other people with whom the girl might have been associated.

Did any one of them—Mrs. Artson-Eskill, Asteteompong, Tete or Wilson-Sarkey—have any reason to make Grace disappear? That was the most important question to be answered.

With regard to Asteteompong, Quarshie's uncle, the Perm Sec, had confirmed that the man had been dismissed from government service. He had been charged by the head of his department with two crimes: adulterating drugs and illegal disposal of those drugs. Only the first charge had been proven, but conviction on that one charge had been sufficient to have him fired. "The man seems to have been altogether too smart for his own well-being," had been the Perm Sec's summary.

So Mrs. Quarshie had volunteered to tackle the problem of finding out more about him by, as she described it, "going in through the back door," meaning that she would visit the convent.

Asteteompong was engaged, in partnership with Mrs. Artson-Eskill, in the production of medicines which were probably of dubious value, except in cash terms to himself, and he must have had considerable contact with Grace. Perhaps the girl had got herself into some sort of position in which he felt threatened by her. Perhaps he wanted some sort of concession from his partner and had kidnapped Grace to hold her as hostage. Perhaps he wanted to use the girl in some scheme and she had run away to escape him. There were many possibilities.

So, Mrs. Quarshie was on her way to carry out her self-imposed task and was already regretting having gotten herself into it. She preferred to work alongside Quarshie rather than independently of him.

And then, to make her anxiety greater, Arimi had also volunteered to carry out a mission: he had suggested that he go with

Kwadoo to the Chobo area around Murder Mountain to ask people there if anyone had ever seen Grace and Professor Wilson-Sarkey in the neighbourhood, and if they had, how recently it had been.

It was a suggestion that Mrs. Quarshie had opposed because, although Arimi was an advanced-for-his-age twelve-year-old and although Kwadoo seemed a reliable associate, the boy's idea of going off into unknown territory made her uneasy.

Quarshie had not scoffed at her concern, but he had reminded her of the excellent work Arimi had done on another case, a few months earlier, when both their lives had depended on his courage and initiative. "He is as capable of taking care of himself," Quarshie had told her, "in almost any situation as you are or I am . . . and I can't believe that, with Kwadoo's muscle behind him, going to some villages and asking a few questions could lead to any serious trouble." In the end it had come down to a case of whether her instincts were more reliable than Quarshie's, and reluctantly, she had allowed herself to be talked out of her concern.

Underneath both these anxieties there was yet a deeper one, of which she was a little ashamed: there was fear in her blood and her genes of men who practiced sorcery. African sorcery was a subject that she had discussed often with Quarshie. She had told him several times that she feared it, and his response had always been the same: he had said that her reaction was a healthy one.

"Necromancy, sorcery, witchcraft and all sorts of other occult practices," he had told her once, "have to do with an addiction men and women have to explore the spiritually unknown. It's a no-man's-land, in which people grope for the good and often find the bad in themselves and in the people around them. Religions also operate in this same area. In both there are disreputable men who claim to have an inside track with the gods or the spirits. Such charlatans take their power from a profound human wish to believe. Then they use this power to manipulate their victims through their innocence and ignorance."

The discussion had taken place in Quarshie's workshop, and he had absentmindedly turned away from her to stare at a piece of carving.

Presently he added, "I believe that humans feed on their emotions. Do you know that? They eat all sorts of spicey foods and drink stimulating beverages to satisfy their appetites for mindless pleasure and excitement. Mostly they are incapable of anything else, incapable of even being able to determine what is healthy or unhealthy for themselves. And sorcerers trade on this self-indulgent thoughtlessness and ignorance."

As Mrs. Quarshie drove out through the fringes of the city, it did occur to her that it was a lot easier to fear dangers like fire that you could see and touch and therefore avoid. The difficult ones to cope with were those which worked in the dark.

Nervously, she admitted to herself that she had very little idea of the kind of traps that Mister Asteteompong might set for her.

By about the same time of the morning that found Mrs. Quarshie leaving Port St. Mary, Arimi, who had not been delayed by other duties, as Mrs. Quarshie had, and Kwadoo were afoot, walking around the base of the Chobo Hills, a rocky outgrowth on the plains which fringed a wide section of the coast. At their highest the rocks stood a little over two thousand feet above the land which surrounded them, and it was one of those peaks which bore the sinister name of Murder Mountain.

Many years earlier the Chobo people, who had existed between two very large and powerful tribes, had taken to the hills as a refuge from the constant slave raids that were directed towards them. The hills, then, had served them well as a fortress, but poorly as the kind of place in which to withstand a siege because there was very little soil. They had been reduced on many occasions to eating rats and making dangerous forays out into their yam and cassava fields in the hope of finding a few tubers that had been left by the enemy.

Murder Mountain was so called because it was a place where those who were convicted of murder were executed by a priest of the Chobo cult. Nearby was Rat Cave, where the murderer's body was left to be disposed of by the rodents. According to Chobo beliefs, a man convicted of murder was ineligible to return to the ancestors. He would move down in the spirit world to become, at best, an ancestor rat.

After the colonial occupation the two competitive tribes had been forced to live at peace with each other. Slavery, also, had been abolished by the colonialists (who had originally profited most from it), so the Chobo people were able to return to cultivate their lands around the foot of the hills without the everlasting fear of being snatched away and transported across the sea to a place where they would be eaten by white men, who, they believed, were all cannibals.

Now, few people were left who lived on the mountain, and most of them served the shrines which abounded there because it had become the holy land of their tribal religion and the seat of all their gods, including those of their ancestors. Clinging to the edges of this sacred territory and hiding in the caves and fissures were the spirits of those who had died "unclean" deaths by natural disaster or in accidents, and also the restless and unhappy spirits of those who were evil and had died because of their lack of respect for the taboos in which their people believed.

From the moment they arrived Arimi and Kwadoo had found the villagers secretive and resentful. At every approach they were greeted by men and women who turned their backs and walked away when they offered any conversation beyond the simplest of greetings and pleasantries.

After a while Kwadoo said, "Catch some humbug here that be too big past all. Nobody fit talk na we." Then breaking back into the language of Port St. Mary, he added, "The ashes are hot only when the fire has been recently tended. But what caused the fire to burn? Even the smoke smells of fear."

Arimi shrugged and replied, "They force us to walk through their silence to find what is on the other side. Those who live at the foot of the mountain may have received information that has upset them from those above. Perhaps the priests will talk because there are none but the gods higher than they are. We must go and see them."

Kwadoo shrugged and said, "A man who is born to be hanged will never be drowned. Do we have the power to control the forces we may meet?"

Arimi said, "We shall proceed without giving offence. We will go showing our respect, without our shirts and carrying our shoes. Even here my father's name is not without those who recognise it. We must buy palm wine to pour libations. Then we shall walk into their holy lands properly prepared." He looked upwards towards the mountain that stretched above the small plinth of rocks on which they stood and added, "We must send a message to Port St. Mary to say we are delayed and must spend the night here. We cannot do what we have to in the time that is left to us, today."

"How will you send a message?"

"By hand. A boy will go on a *trotro* with some paper I will give him. I will pay his fare. They will pay him for the paper when he gets to the clinic. I shall tell them to do that in what I write."

"For a young cockerel you crow very loudly."

To Arimi the words were said censoriously enough to sound like a challenge to his authority.

By local custom a boy of Arimi's age should never look a man as much his senior as Kwadoo straight and steadily in the eye, but that is what he did. Very coolly, without any suggestion of anger, he told the taxi driver, "Perhaps you would like to take the message, yourself, in your car, while I proceed with what I have to do."

His defiance was so perfectly judged that Kwadoo could do nothing but admire the way it was done and smile.

He said, "Send the boy. We will go on the mountain together, though your mother will not be pleased either with you or with me."

Mrs. Quarshie, at that moment, was not very pleased with herself.

Gaining entrance to the convent had not proved difficult. She had obtained the name of the senior of the elderly women who ran it from her one-time pupil and simply drove to the door of the compound and asked to see her. When they met they discovered that each, in her own way, was a person of authority, and then, having recognised it, treated each other accordingly.

Mrs. Quarshie's objective this time was a wish to see the training of the girls with a view towards accepting some of them to work in the clinic.

West African convents differ in almost every way from European convents—except that those who enter both institutions are female and both are concerned, to a greater or lesser degree, with religion.

Of the differences the first is that novices enter West African convents before they reach the age of puberty. Then one of the main objects of the training is to make those who attend it suitable to be exemplary wives, girls for whom their fathers can command a high bride price. So they are taught to dance, to weave, to sing, to make pots, to sew, to cook and to buy and sell in the market. Also, instead of being swathed up to the tips of their chins and down to their ankles with yards of cloth, they go naked except for a few beads around their waists which support a strip of red cloth that is passed between their legs. The rest of their apparel serves as decoration. They wear more beads around their legs, which are also adorned with small bells. They have bracelets and necklaces of beads, and headbands made of rushes interwoven with red parrot feathers. They also wear, over one shoulder, a woven band of rushes coated with a magic preparation that protects the wearers against people who may have bad intentions towards them.

Beyond all other objectives at West African convents, however, it is the purpose to establish in the girl a firm respect for the taboos of both the gods of the cult to which the convent belongs and to the taboos of the clan. It is said that when they leave the convent they should be "as nice in their hearts and souls as they are beautiful in their bodies." In short, they are taught to be worthy members of their church and model wives and mothers at the same time.

Mrs. Quarshie was not at the moment pleased with herself because though she had been shown all the activities in the convent she had found nothing except Asteteompong's name, as a religious instructor, to connect him with the convent and nothing that was even faintly out of the ordinary in the way the place was run.

Then two things happened. On a shelf in one room she saw an array of medicine bottles which were in the charge of a young man who tried to snatch a bottle away from her when she picked one up to look at it closely.

His behaviour made Mrs. Quarshie glance with surprise towards the old woman who had conducted her around the convent. Immediately the young man was fiercely scolded and ordered from the room. In response he muttered something in an ugly tone under his breath, but he moved away only as far as the door, where he remained and watched her.

The label on the first bottle she picked up read:

ASTETEOMPONG'S ELIXIR. Underneath those words was written:

The only perfect tonic for pregnant women. Guaranteed to protect the child in the womb against mishap while it is being carried and after birth. It also prevents constipation, reduces giddiness, vomiting, backache, loss of appetite and energy. Essential to all women who want to bear healthy, clever and happy children. Start taking it as soon as you miss your first menstrual period.

Mrs. Quarshie set the bottle down on the shelf, resisting an impulse to smash it on the floor. Then, with the beginnings of a plan forming in her mind, she picked up another bottle. On this one she read:

ASTETEOMPONG'S MAGIC SKIN DISEASE CURE

An unbeatable treatment for all kinds of rashes and skin sores. It also sharpens failing eyesight. Taken internally, it gives added potency to men and increases the pleasure wives can obtain from their relationship with their husbands. A sovereign remedy for those who have previously suffered from abortion. Try it and prove its wonderful efficiency for yourself.

With slow deliberation and without any comment she returned the bottle to its place, glanced along the rest of the shelf and said something noncommittal to her guide. She had mastered the fury the first sight of Asteteompong's quack medicines had roused in her, and she had made the decision to confront Asteteompong and threaten him with exposure if he did not cooperate with their investigation.

She thanked her guide ceremoniously, congratulated her on the excellence of the convent, got into her car and started the engine.

It was then that the second significant event occurred.

The car had just started to move when the door, on the passenger side, was flung open and the young man who had tried to snatch the bottle out of her hand threw himself into the seat beside her.

Instinctively Mrs. Quarshie put her foot on the brake, and at virtually the same moment she felt a painful prick between her third and fourth ribs. Glancing sideways, she saw that the young man was pressing the point of a long slender knife against her.

In a low voice he said, "It will go right to the heart, ma, if I press any further."

Forcing the words past a constriction in her throat, Mrs. Quarshie asked, "What do you want?"

"You will drive to Mister Asteteompong's home. He told me that if you came to the convent I was to bring you to see him. Holding the knife like this, ma, makes me feel nervous, and I don't want to press harder by mistake, so make you please do what I tell you."

Trying to sound nonchalant as she complied with the young man's order, Mrs. Quarshie said, "I was going to see Mister Asteteompong anyway, so you can put the knife away."

"No, ma. I keep the knife like this until my master tells me to put it away."

Not so nonchalantly Mrs. Quarshie asked, "Did Mister Asteteompong dip it in anything before he gave it to you?" Sorcerers were known to have access to very virulent poisons.

The youth said, "He never tell me, ma."

It was a simple statement that might have filled Mrs. Quarshie with terror if she had not reached a stage in which, at least superficially, her principal feeling had become one of fatalism.

During one change of gears she was conscious of the tip of the knife grating against bone, and she could feel a trickle of warm blood, like a trickle of sweat, running down her side. For a moment she had to fight to overcome an onset of faintness.

Getting out of the car when they reached their destination was very difficult. Her attacker insisted that she climb past the gear lever and get out of the car on his side, so that he could continue to keep the knife pricking her ribs. It meant, in fact, that he punctured her skin two or three times.

Asteteompong was not in his curtained office when they got there and had to be sent for. Rather shakily now Mrs. Quarshie asked if she could sit down because she felt that she was about to lose control of her knees. She knew too that from the coldness of her hands and feet and the rapid rate of her pulse beating in her ears that she might easily collapse altogether.

In as strong a voice as she could muster she warned the young man, "If I don't sit down, or preferably lie down, I shall probably faint."

Her captor frowned with the effort he made to come to a decision, then said, "Lie on the floor." He even helped her down while still keeping the knife close to her chest. When she was flat on her back, and as waves of nausea swept over her and the young man held his knife against her chest just below her left breast, Asteteompong walked in.

Mrs. Quarshie was bleeding severely enough for the side of her uniform to be stained a dark red and for a small pool of blood to have started to form on the wooden boards beside her.

Asteteompong's reaction was cool and deliberate.

To the boy he said, "You can put away the knife and leave."

To Mrs. Quarshie he said, "I hope the wound is superficial. Will you allow me to examine it and dress it?"

Arimi found the emptiness of the grey rocky spaces which surrounded him very lonely, even though he had Kwadoo struggling up the steep scree behind him.

Rather than trying to scale or work around the boulders which lay in their path they had decided to keep to a loose, tumbled swath of smaller rocks and shale that had originated in a landslide, because other climbers had left a rudimentary footpath which zigzagged backwards and forwards across the slope. The remains of a nearby tree stripped of its bark and leaves stood skeletal and bleached to bone white. Above them the clouds were so heavy with the water they had picked up out at sea that they leaked in a curious way, depositing, every now and then, nut-sized blobs of water which exploded when they hit anything. Another remarkable thing about these globules of water was that they were warm.

So far Arimi had not seen a hut of any sort, or even a cave.

Presently he found a shallow patch of shelter under the edge of a projecting boulder and paused to rest, turning to face back the way they had come. With a sudden feeling of wonder he saw a vulture sweep past on motionless wings, its primaries spread like fingers on a hand. It was *below* him.

As Kwadoo came up to him he said, "I see with the eye of a bird. It is wonderful."

Kwadoo shook his head. "We share this land and this view with the old ones." He meant the dead. "And it is dangerous. They are not of our people, and may punish us because we walk on their land uninvited. It is said, also, that the unclean dead inhabit here. They may come between us and cause us to lose each other.

Arimi said, "If that happens, find a way that looks towards the sea and descend towards it."

"And at night?"

"There will be the lights of the city even though they may be far away."

When they started to climb again, they had to leave the tongue of rubble that had formed the landslide, and soon came to the remains of a village. If the rock face itself had been lonely, here the feeling was of total desolation. It troubled Kwadoo particularly because it was so easy to imagine the ruins to be occupied by phantoms that might drift through the shattered doors, travel footlessly over the rubble, climb like smoke through the broken roofs or lay concealed in the cracked and drunkenly heeling grain-storage bins that were shaped like young pine cones and had once stood on stilts to keep them free from rats. They had had charms tied around the legs of the cradle in which they stood. The rats were supposed to recognise the charms as containing magic properties that would destroy them.

Still there were no signs of human life.

Kwadoo said, "If a storm breaks we shall be inside it, where the gods make the lightning."

It was a fearful thought until Arimi found the answer: "Those who lived here in the past must often have known that experience and survived it."

"But," objected Kwadoo, "they had their own gods beside them to defend them." He was determined not to be comforted.

Then as they climbed onwards, with their heads down, they were frightened, suddenly, to hear a voice addressing them.

Looking up, they found an old man standing a little above them. He spoke a language they did not understand, and they answered him with greetings in the language of the people of Port St. Mary.

He replied in the same tongue. His greeting was curt and followed by an equally curt command.

"Abrechi," he said, naming one of the local gods, "does not want you on the mountain. You should leave it by the way you came."

"Why, father?" Arimi asked. "Why may we not walk on the mountain? We go shirtless in respect and we have palm wine to pour as libation."

"Boy, the eye that sees can never see itself. It is impossible to know some things, for Abrechi will not answer questions concerning them. Only do his bidding or you will anger him."

Kwadoo had turned immediately the old man had relayed Abrechi's order and was walking back down the hill.

Arimi wanted to protest again, but without Kwadoo to support him he had not the courage to do so.

When they had gone a little way Kwadoo called back over his shoulder, "It is well that we obey and have no palaver with Abrechi. Pour a libation now and ask for his goodwill, that we may be able to get to the village safely."

Arimi complied, but then as they continued down the mountain, he allowed Kwadoo to get farther and farther ahead.

When several hundred yards separated them Arimi moved quickly away to one side, dropped flat on his stomach behind a boulder and, on his hands and knees, continued to creep away from the line they had taken on their ascent and descent of the mountain.

Kwadoo, determined to get clear of any malevolent intentions that Abrechi might have towards him, did not look back for almost ten minutes. He thought that Arimi would be feeling the same way, and when he did turn and look back and found that the boy was no longer in sight his immediate reaction was that the god had stolen him away to show his displeasure.

It was the beginning of an unhappy night for Kwadoo. Not only had he lost the boy, but he knew now that he loved him and he dared not return to Port St. Mary without him to face the Quarshies. Also he knew that, with all his muscle, he would be powerless in any confrontation with Abrechi. He would have to obtain the support of another god before he went on the mountain again. He did not know which one, however, and the people in the village would not talk to him.

There had been no alternative open to Mrs. Quarshie other than to accept Asteteompong's offer to dress her wounds. Three were little more than pricks, but one needed serious treatment. Asteteompong put sulphonamide powder on all of them before covering them with dressings that he fixed in place with surgical tape.

He worked neatly and quickly, talking as he did so. "I told the boy to use the knife as a threat," he told her. "I certainly had no intention that he should injure this beautiful skin. I am afraid I am going to have to get rid of him. He's not very clever. Anyway, it's nice to see you again, Prudence, even if your interest in my affairs is becoming tiresome. Now what are we going to do with all these bloodstains on your clothes? Perhaps"—there was a salacious gleam in his eye—"you would like to take them off so that I can get someone to wash them. You can lie on my bed in there while you wait for them to dry. . . . No? Too bad. And then you were saying the other day that you want a baby. You tempt me, Prudence, indeed you do."

Mrs. Quarshie closed her eyes and prayed for the help she needed to deal with this man.

He had finished the dressings, and she said:

"We won't worry about the bloodstains. At least not at the moment. Though they may cause you some trouble when I show them to my husband.

Asteteompong shook his head. "Let me help you up," he said. And a moment later, "There, be careful how you sit so that you don't start that wound bleeding again."

Then, as he seated himself, he said, "I am not afraid of your husband, Prudence. Though I would like to know, I admit, why he and you are so interested in my affairs. Might we not make more headway in our relationship if you tell me?"

"Will you bring your boy back in again with his knife if I don't?"

"I could. I could also arrange for you to have a rather nasty accident going back down the scarp. It is a long drop off that road. But we don't need to talk about such unpleasant extremes as that. Why don't you just give me a chance to answer a direct question about whatever it is that has set you spying on me?"

"All right. What do you know about Grace Artson-Eskill's disappearance?"

Astetemopong frowned and then said, "Has she disappeared? And if she has, why should I know anything about it?"

"You know her pretty well?"

"I have been acquainted with her since she was a child. And you says she has disappeared. Not just left home? She does not get along very well with her mother, you know." And he frowned and asked, "In any case, why should I be concerned? I don't think she liked me much better than she liked her mother. And, yes, I have tried to persuade her to let me share her bed. She is fairly free with such invitations but I . . . Shall we say I am not her type?"

"Who is?"

"That snake-hipped footballer."

"And . . . ?"

"Oh, I don't know . . . there are others. She is a beautiful girl. What about that man from the University, Wilson-Sarkey? She has been around with him a lot lately."

Mrs. Quarshie looked at the sorcerer very levelly but said nothing.

Asteteompong told her, "You have beautiful eyes, Prudence . . . and you don't believe me?"

"It would make it a lot easier if I did."

"So what are you going to do about your suspicions?"

Mrs. Quarshie lifted her chin and said bluntly, "I have more than suspicions about those patent medicines you make and sell. The Permanent Secretary at the Department of Internal Affairs is a close relative. He has your file on his desk now. The police could start an investigation into your affairs that could last a long time, be very damaging and probably end in criminal proceedings being taken against you."

For the first time Asteteompong lost a little of his suavity.

He hesitated before he asked, "So?"

Mrs. Quarshie got up from her chair without answering. Ignoring the question, she said, "I am going to return to Port St. Mary. I want to be home in time to go to a meeting of the Akhana Women's Association."

As she reached the door she turned back to the man who was sitting behind his desk looking after her with a partly anxious, partly puzzled expression on his face and added, "I think I shall recommend that my husband come up next time to see you, perhaps accompanied by his uncle, the Perm Sec. After our . . . meeting today I am sure they will have questions they will want to ask you."

She closed the door quietly behind her. It might help, she thought, to let him stew in his own juice for a while.

It was very cold. Much colder than Arimi had thought it would be. Since he had left Kwadoo he had moved stealthily up the mountain, even continuing after dark, keeping the loom of the lights from Port St. Mary immediately behind him.

He had begun to feel afraid and to wish he had had Kwadoo with him as soon as the black hood of the night dropped onto the distant rim of the sea.

His fear increased to terror when the owls started to call. They were known to be the familiars of witches, if not witches themselves.

The mountain was, in fact, a natural habitat for owls because of its large population of mice and rats, a fact, Arimi felt, that might be found in a textbook, but unfortunately there were no textbook explanations of why old women became dangerous witches and flew around at night in the bodies of owls.

From the way the owls were calling, as he listened to them, they seemed to have him surrounded.

The clouds had lifted and cleared, and in the dim light of a waning moon the rocks took on menacing shapes. Several times Arimi thought he observed someone, or something, moving in their shadows. Once he saw, quite clearly, a rat run across a piece of ground from one area of blackness to another.

Presently a new dimension of anxiety filled his little universe. For some reason the villagers set fire to the scrub around the base of the mountain and the many small savannah-bred trees which encompassed its rocky prominence. Acrid smoke climbed the slopes toward Arimi like the creeping fingers of a blind man seeking a handhold on the rocks. Through gaps in the dark columns he could see the red and orange light of flames illuminating the grey cottony balls of smoke at ground level.

Now and then sparks fountained high into the sky and the wind carried the sound of drumming.

Arimi, just before school had recessed for the holidays, had been doing some reading in elementary geology, and to him it looked and felt as if the Chobo Hills were afloat in a small lake of molten lava.

He was shivering as much from fear as from the suddenly chill atmosphere, and like a little frightened animal, he sought somewhere to hide.

Soon, still climbing, he came to a hut.

By putting his ear against the closed door he could hear someone inside breathing deeply and regularly, but he was afraid to disturb whoever it was in case it made them angry. At the same time he was afraid to go away and break the contact he seemed to have made with another human. He stole quietly around the hut to see if there was any other access to it and found none. Its one window was closed with heavy shutters. However, just beneath the window there was a hollow in the ground. When he lay down there, close to the wall, he could still hear snores and the occasional rustling of a mat as someone moved on it, and he was grateful for the feeling of human companionship these sounds provided. Curling up with his knees almost under his chin, he lay, without knowing it, as he had once lain in his mother's womb. What he did know was that he felt more or less protected and, because he was out of the damp wind, a little less cold. He was also very tired and quickly went to sleep.

When he awoke it was dawn, and against the pale sky he saw, standing beyond his feet looking down at him, the silhouette of a woman, grotesquely warped with age.

She was wrapped against the cold in an old cloth which was twisted around her body and hooded her forehead. She also held it across the lower part of her face with one hand.

The smoke of the night before had cleared, but the air was still tinged by its smell, though that was almost completely smothered by a sickening odour of putrescence.

At first Arimi thought it came from the old woman, but he soon realised that it was far too pervasive for that.

The old woman pointed a bent skinny finger at him and said something in a language he could not understand.

In a shaky voice and in the language of the people of Port St. Mary, Arimi responded by asking timidly, "Are you a witch?"

The old woman stared at him for a long time from beneath heavily drooping eyelids. She ignored his question, which she evidently understood, for in the same language she asked him a question of her own.

"Have you led others to me who are suffering from the hot breath?" she asked.

"I . . . I don't know what you speak of, mother. What is the hot breath?"

"You are not of my people. Why are you here? Why are you here, lying like a snake coiled in the grass, beside my hut?"

"I am seeking information, mother."

"You are not of my people. You say you don't know anything of the hot breath and you lie curled by my house like a snake. Who are you? Who sent you? And what do you want?"

As she spoke Arimi was almost overwhelmed by the stench which came to him on a light puff of wind.

"What is that smell, mother?" It was so strong he could think of nothing else.

"Woodsmoke. They are fighting the hot breath down there, boy."

"No. There is another smell."

"If there is, it does not come to me. Is that the information you are seeking?"

"No, mother. I am seeking a man and a woman. A man in his

middle years and a young woman. They are book-learned people, mother, not as you and me, simple people."

"You are not simple; I can see inside you. You are afraid. Perhaps the smell you ask of is that of the hot breath. All who smell that fear it greatly."

"Mother, they were two strangers and they would have come here asking about the past."

"There are many who do that. Even some Anglis." She was speaking of the English. "The dead hate their questions. It is just the same as if these questioners came into my house and handled everything in it and asked questions about everything. There have been some here who would have examined my body if I would have let them. They all want to know too much. And when it gets to be the same for the ancestors, breaking up their graves and giving them no peace, then I wish that Abrechi would order these inquisitive people to be killed and left in the cave for the rats."

"And the two I spoke of, mother?"

"What of them? Perhaps they came, perhaps they didn't. Either way they would be none of my business, nor should they be. Now, go before the priests find you here and call on Abrechi to punish you. And, boy, as you pass downwards beware of the hot breath, for it has a great hunger and the young and tender often fall prey to it."

. . . and it speaks at one and the same time of perversion, corruption and putrefaction. It is a malignity, a primal sickness which can permeate and infect the soul of a man to the deepest measure of his being.

CHAPTER NINE

"Doctor Quarshie Baffled."

Arimi said, "I met again with Kwadoo when I got down to the bottom of the hill. Still, people were reluctant to speak with him, or with me, but everyone was very troubled, and it seemed to me that some were packing their things to leave. And there was talk of the hot breath there, too."

"You should not have gone up that mountain alone. Anything could have happened to you," Mrs. Quarshie told him.

"No one stuck any knives in me, m'ma."

Quarshie grinned and said, "But you were frightened witless if I understand what you are saying correctly."

"Yes, I was very frightened, sir. And the smell . . ."

"Tell us about that again."

"There is nothing to tell except that it nearly made me sick."

"You don't know what could have caused it?"

Arimi paused and then said, "Bad meat, sir."

"Where exactly were you on the mountain?"

"I don't know, sir. But I could find the way back there again."

"You don't think the smell came from the old woman, or her hut?"

"No, m'ma. It was too big for that. It was everywhere."

"Did she say it had anything to do with this thing you say she kept calling the 'hot breath'?"

"No, sir."

It was late in the morning of the day Kwadoo, with great relief, had brought Arimi back from their venture.

Mrs. Quarshie said, "Well, you have talked long enough. You had better go and take a shower, eat a good lunch and then go and rest for a while."

"But, m'ma, I'm all right, I—"

Quarshie said softly, "It will be better if you do as Prudence says. A skilled warrior never uses up his energy between engagements. To preserve your strength for the next skirmish you must eat and sleep."

Arimi looked rebellious, fought a battle with himself and said, "Yes, sir," and left the room.

When he was out of earshot Quarshie said, "'The hot breath,' did you ever hear of that before, Prudence?"

"No. I suppose it has something to do with witchcraft. That could also account for the uneasiness of the people in the villages around the mountain. It would make things a lot more simple if the same witchcraft practices were common to all our tribes instead of each one having beliefs and practices of their own."

"Or if," Quarshie suggested, "there was a simple set of rules to describe the way witchcraft works. I don't agree, though, that what is happening amongst the Chobo is witchcraft. I think it is bad medicine. Witchcraft, in my experience, has no rites, no invocations or drumbeating involved with it. It is simply the work of wicked people, or of people who have some aberration, using autosuggestion or some similar power that we don't yet understand. It is believed, particularly by the witches, that they can harm people simply by wishing harm on them." He paused, then added, "Perhaps we should, however, look into what is happening amongst the Chobo, but not for the moment because there is nothing to relate what Arimi tells us is going on there to our search for Grace. While I do, in fact, have something that seems to have quite a direct bearing on it. It was brought to me at the surgery this morning."

He got up from his chair and crossed to the table which carried his doctor's bag. From it he produced a fat envelope. As he sat down again he continued, "If I am to believe what is in here, our job is over and Grace is safe and well in Grande Banane. See what you make of it. First there is an anonymous covering letter." He sorted the papers until he found it, and read:

> *The enclosed documents may be of interest to you. They will prove that you are being misled.*

"You can see that the person who put that message together used the old device of cutting the words out of a printed text. Usually it is done with a newspaper. This time, from the quality of the paper,

I think it was a book. It is signed, 'A WELL WISHER,' in capital letters, each one cut out separately. And there were four enclosures. The first I am going to read to you has an address in Grande Banane and is dated two days after Grace is supposed to have disappeared. I am meant to believe that it is from her and it is addressed to Tete. It reads:

"*My handsome lover. It will surprise you, perhaps, to hear from me from Grande Banane. You must come to see me here as soon as you can. I cannot stay at home anymore because I am afraid that if I do, either I will kill my mother or she will kill me. You know how it is between us.*

"*Mon chéri, do you remember what I taught you that meant? Mon chéri, I want you and need you . . . so come soon.*

Je te raffole,
Grace."

Quarshie showed the letter to his wife. As she looked at it he said, "It seems simple and engaging enough to be true, but when I checked around a bit there are a couple of details which make it suspect. The first is the address. You have met Isutu, the Director of Posts and Telegraphs in Grande Banane. As you know, we were in Montreal together. I phoned him and asked him to check out who lives at the address she gives, Rue de Marien Ngouabi, 23. He called me back and told me that the address no longer exists. Ngouabi, after whom the street was named, has been dead quite a long time and it is now called Rue de Moktar Ould Daddah.

"The second point is that none of the airlines has any record of a passenger called Grace Artson-Eskill travelling on any of the dates she would have had to travel had she left on the day Tete last saw her and before the date she wrote the letter. She could, I suppose, have travelled with an assumed name and risked the immigration people in Banane noticing it. There is no other way she could have got to Banane in under two days except by flying.

"So those two points suggest that the letter might be a red herring designed to confuse us. On the other hand its general tone seems reasonable enough, and there is one other little point which might suggest that it is genuine. The *e* in *chéri* carries an acute accent as part of the type face, so it would have had to be typed on a typewriter designed to be used by francophones. They are few and far between here in Akhana, though I suppose they exist at the Embassy and maybe at the offices of the French or Swiss trading companies.

"Frankly I am suspicious of it, and on the evidence of the other documents I have here I think I am meant to be suspicious."

Quarshie smiled at his wife's look of bewilderment.

"I think we are up against a mind that works in a tortuous way. I expect you will be of the same opinion when you hear the rest of the evidence.

"This"—he held up another sheet of paper—"is apparently a photocopy of a page from Grace's diary. It reads, 'Tete was asking for money again this evening. What do I do? I am at the man's mercy. His amazing virility is the only thing mother and I are agreed upon. He is the most splendid jockey. To be ridden by him is to be ridden by a master. The only hold I have is that he knows that I could make trouble for him with my enslaved mama. I am permitted a piece of the action by her only on the understanding that she has priority, but in fact, he is contemptuous of her. For fun one day I made a tape recording of our exchanges on my mat before, during and after one of our rides together. Then I made a copy of the tape in a written form and gave it to him. He did not know that I had the tape recorder running. The beginning of the transcript, a recording of the mare urging the jockey to exceed his previous efforts, amused him. Then came a piece in which he compared our performance with the kind of thing that happened with my mother, and he was furious knowing that he had played right into my hands. Besides paying him she has some other kind of hold on him. He has never told me what it is, *but* if she ever heard that tape, all the terrible, laughable, grotesque things he says about her, he would not only lose all the money she pays him and he uses to bet on the football games in which he plays—he has told me that when he can get the right odds he sometimes bets on his opponents and then blows the game by shooting wide—but he would also be inviting her to take the terrible retribution she apparently has in store for him.'"

Mrs. Quarshie said, "What a charming family, and as for Tete . . . Why don't we give up the case?"

Her husband looked at her sombrely. "That was my thought, too. We are digging in a manure heap. That is, if all this is true." And then more slowly he added, "And that is what we have to establish first—that and whether Grace has run away, been kidnapped or—murdered."

"You mean that amongst monsters we have to decide which is the worst?"

Quarshie frowned and told her, "We are not at the bottom of the manure heap yet. We have another excerpt from this young woman's diary."

He put a different sheet of paper on top of the others and read, "'Odu—that, I have found out is Wilson-Sarkey's first name—Odu is having trouble with his wife. He is as enchanted with my performance in bed as I am with Tete's. The man is mad about me. So, it is really rather funny. For taking his pleasure with me I make him pay the fee Tete charges me, or else, I have told him, I will give his wife all the evidence she needs to divorce him. She is a rich and suspicious woman. He is doing some very good research: he has found evidence in the Chobo Hills of some early iron age inhabitants. They were, Odu says, smelting iron there before they were smelting it in Europe. But it is her money which pays for the research. So, of course, he does not want to get divorced and lose his "funding," as he calls it. So if he can use her money to pay for his work why shouldn't he use it to pay for his pleasure?'"

"Who can have sent you all this stuff? It involves everyone we are looking at except . . ."

"Except?" Quarshie wanted to know.

Mrs. Quarshie touched her ribs gingerly and said, "Except Asteteompong."

"Precisely, and that worries me."

"Because you think he may have sent it to you?"

"No. I told you that the person—who would by the way have to be Mrs. A.E.—who sent all this has a devious mind. I think the intention could be quite the reverse: to make me suspicious of Asteteompong. All four of them know we have some sort of suspicion of them, so someone is shuffling the cards in an effort to confuse us."

"Well, they have certainly confused me. How did the envelope get to your office?"

"It was brought by a little boy from the market who said he was told he would be paid for delivering it. On the envelope was written, 'The contents concern Grace Artson-Eskill.'"

"Did the boy tell you anything about whoever it was who gave the envelope to him?"

"I refused to pay him until he did. He told me it was a stranger from the zongo. The description he gave me would fit eight out of ten Northerners."

"Who of the people we are looking at has a devious mind?"

Quarshie's smile was rueful. "All of them. But this afternoon I am going to start back with number one, Mrs. A.E."

At that moment Hassan, the steward, came in carrying the Port St. Mary *Evening News.* He gave it to Quarshie, saying, "Some doctah man send dis for mastah. I look um catch big pictsah for mastah for front side."

Quarshie took the paper from the man's hand. The front page held a picture which ran to half its depth and was three columns wide, showing him crouching down talking to a small girl. Over the picture the caption read, "Doctor Quarshie Baffled." Beneath it, in the paper's best condensed gothic, was a statement which read:

This paper has received a hot tip that our famous Doctor
Quarshie is working on a case that has him completely
mystified. We are not able at this moment to go into
any further details, but we shall be watching the great
man's actions very closely and bring you reports on whom
he sees, what he does and where he goes. So get the
Evening News regularly and learn from the Doctor's example
just what it takes to track down a criminal and bring
him, or it might be her, to justice.

Quarshie put the paper down and laughed.

"What does it mean?" Mrs. Quarshie asked. "What is going on?"

"I don't know, but I can make a good guess. Not only is someone trying to confuse the issue but he is trying to make it impossible for me to operate."

"Well, the newspaper must know who it is. You must phone the editor."

"I will, but I don't expect to learn anything that will help. Whoever the informant is will certainly have covered his trail."

He went to the telephone, looked up the number and dialled.

After a moment he said, "Yes. This is Doctor Quarshie. I want to talk to the editor, or if he is not available to whoever is on the desk." There was a pause, then he said, "Good afternoon. . . . Yes. . . . Oh, he left a message for me? He listened for some moments, then said, "I understand. Well, tell him if I find reporters interfering with my freedom of action I will arrange, through the Department of Internal Affairs, to have them put where they won't be able to interfere with anyone or anything except the cockroaches that will be keeping them company. I am told the prisons abound with them. You have that? . . . Good. Thank you." He hung up.

To Mrs. Quarshie he said, "As I thought. The tip was anonymous. However, to convince the editor that it was not a hoax the caller said he would arrange for the delivery of a considerable amount of money which the paper could keep and give to a charity if it found that it was false information. I spoke with the news editor, who said that they had nothing to lose by trying it. The editor-in-chief said that if the lead was a bad one he would give half the money to one of your maternity and child welfare clinics."

"And put the other half into his pocket," Mrs. Quarshie snorted scornfully. "So what are you going to do?"

Quarshie went and stood looking out at the louring sky, the red earth driveway which led up to the bungalow and the rocketing shoots of brilliant mauve, orange and red bougainvillea which lined it. In the oppressive afternoon heat everything was still and silent.

Presently he said, "First I am going to try to catch Mrs. A.E. at home. If I phone and ask for an appointment she will put me off or arrange to meet me at the leper colony again. I want to see how she lives and have a look at Grace's room. I have not suggested that before because I believed she would say no, but now I have enough information to push my way in if I have to. Afterwards I will go and get hold of the editor of the *Evening News* and have a little heart-to-heart talk with him." There was a tone in Quarshie's voice which Mrs. Quarshie recognised. It meant that he had reached a level of resolve that would increase the impetus of his activities to a point where he would drive himself and everybody else associated with him to the brink of exhaustion.

CHAPTER TEN

*"If you think that a parrot cannot
bleed, then look at its red tail."*

Mrs. Artson-Eskill's house was an affair of terraces and balconies which stood on a slope at the top of the scarp looking out across the road to the coastal plain and, in the far distance, the sea. So its terraces stepped backwards up the hill to the front of the house, where the balconies, three of them, one above the other, stood, like the rungs of a ladder, attached. The driveway zigzagged up the side of the terracing to the main entrance. To Quarshie the house had the air of a concrete fortress, and he half expected to see the front windows being used as gunports.

The little girl, Rosebud, whom he had met at the leper colony, answered the door. Though many adults regarded Quarshie's appearance as forbidding, this was seldom the case with children, and Rosebud was no exception. She knew, instinctively, that the big man was on her side against a world that was otherwise not very kind to her.

She said in a subdued little voice, "You are welcome, sah," when she saw him. "I will tell moddah you are here."

Quarshie put his hand gently on her shoulder and said, "No, I will announce myself. Which room is moddah in?"

"Ee be dat one, sah." She pointed to a closed door. Quarshie walked across the hall, which was obviously used as a waiting room because it had benches along the walls, and knocked on the door.

The reply he received was a barked, "Who's that?"

Quarshie opened the door and said, "Your humble servant, moddah."

Mrs. Artson-Eskill was wearing glasses with lenses that looked as big as car headlights. The way they magnified her eyes exaggerated her expression of surprise. She took them off and said furiously, "How did you get in here?"

"The usual way," Quarshie replied, "through the front door—and don't take your fury out on that child who opened it for me because I am a little bigger than she is and she could not have stopped me if she had tried."

Another office opened out of Mrs. Artson-Eskill's in which a young man and a young woman were both busy, or making a show of being busy, at their typewriters. Neither of them was actually striking the keys because had they been doing so they would not have been able to hear what was going on next door.

Glowering at her visitor, Mrs. Artson-Eskill stood up and said, "We will go into another room." And led the way past Quarshie back into the hallway and up a stairway at the end of it.

Following her, Quarshie watched the working of Mrs. Artson-Eskill's vast haunches and wondered at the strength of her pelvic girdle and the rest of her bone structure as it carried its two-hundred-and-fifty-pound load of flesh up the steep concrete steps.

When they reached the top she was breathing a little hard, but in fact, Quarshie thought, her indignation could have accounted for that.

The lounge into which she led him was furnished in a way that would have allowed it to meet the needs of a herd of elephants, so sturdily were all the chairs and davenports built.

Anticipating any comments, Mrs. Artson-Eskill said over her shoulder, "The only ready-made furniture you can buy is built of matchwood. I have everything specially made. You are one of the few visitors who will appreciate being able to sit down without having everything groan under you." Then she suddenly turned and faced him, blocking his path, so that they were standing touching each other. "I have also had my bed constructed to support a big woman and a big man. But that wouldn't interest you. Or would it?"

Quarshie smiled and told her, "Well, it is not the reason for my visit."

"Of course, I would have been surprised if you had said yes. I have heard you described as an uxorious man." Her tone was slightly contemptuous. "So, why have you come barging in here? Sit down. Sit down."

"To report on the work I am doing on your behalf."

"Have you found the girl? Or any trace of her?"

"No."

"So what is there to report?"

"That you and she used to fight fiercely, and that she had been heard to say that she hated you. Also that you and she were sharing the attentions of the same man, which would suggest that you might have been jealous of her."

"You are contemptible, contemptible. Get out of this house." The words were noisy but lacked authority or any real depth of feeling.

Quarshie did not move.

Mrs. Artson-Eskill also sat quite still, with her eyes closed.

The silence which followed lasted a long time. Presently Quarshie saw a tear run down Mrs. Artson-Eskill's face and hang poised as a drip under one of her chins. He suggested, in a softer tone of voice, "I thought you should know what might come out in the evidence if we don't find Grace and the case comes into court."

Mrs. Artson-Eskill sniffed and, without opening her eyes, said, "You thought nothing of the sort. You enjoy biting the hand that-feeds you. You are like all the rest—Tete, that cheap witch doctor, my late unlamented husband and even Grace, who inherited my brains but not my ambitions."

She opened her eyes and the tear fell off onto the surge of flesh that disappeared into the top of her dress.

"What about Professor Wilson-Sarkey? Would you include him as well? He was your husband's protégé, wasn't he?"

It was a shot in the dark that scored.

Mrs. Artson-Eskill nodded her head.

"All of them, every one. I use my wits to earn good money and they all steal it from me. I say steal because in my eyes when you take something and don't give anything back you steal. Even Tete laughs at me behind my back. If you know that Grace and I were sharing a man you must know that he was the one."

"Was Asteteompong ever one of your lovers?"

"Of course he was. How do you think he got the money to start that dirty business of his? Oh, I heard that your wife had been to see him. There is nothing that happens here in Adaja that I don't hear about. If my money does nothing else for me at least it keeps me well informed. You are not serious about suspecting me of having anything to do with Grace's disappearance?"

Quarshie shook his head and said, "I can't give you a categorical 'no' to that question. Not yet. I still have to gather a lot more information before I am prepared to commit myself in any way. It is a lazy cat that eats dead mice."

"You are wasting your time and my money by continuing to investigate me. Would I have called in the best criminal investigator in the country and paid him to prove that I am the culprit?"

Quarshie moved, trying to find a more comfortable position in his chair, and replied, "Prove to me, Mrs. Artson-Eskill, that you are not the culprit. Start by telling me what you think the culprit is guilty of."

"Grace has disappeared."

"How do you know? I mean, how did you come to the conclusion that she had not just gone off on her own, say, to Grande Banane? I know she left you a note. You told me that before. But what made you believe it?"

It was Mrs. Artson-Eskill's turn to move uneasily in her chair.

Presently she sighed and said, "Because she telephoned me the day after she left and told me she would not be coming back."

"Why didn't you tell me that before?"

"Would you have believed me? Do you believe me now?"

Quarshie shrugged. "I doubt that you can support your statement with any solid evidence. Never mind; I will let it stand for the moment. You have said several times that Grace was rebellious. You and she fought. What was the real issue? Do you hate her?"

Again Mrs. Artson-Eskill closed her eyes and sat silent for a time. Presently she said, "It is terrible to think that you need to ask a question of that sort of a child's mother. Of course I don't hate her. Nor do I expect you to believe me when I say I love her, though it happens to be true." She looked intently at her questioner. "She is a very clever girl, Doctor. The trouble is that though the blood tie is strong we stand on opposite sides of a fence. We live in different worlds. I represent a threat, *the* threat to everything that she would like to believe in. I see myself as representing what is *true* and as being modern and realistic. In the past our people lived communally. They could do that because their survival depended on sharing and their values were simple. In our society, today, survival is very much more difficult because we live in a different forest, a thicker one than we ever thought could exist. That means that we have to fight harder to cut our way through it and it is very much more difficult to see where we are going, and it's clear that we shan't be able to get anywhere together in a mob. So it is each man for himself. We can't do what Grace wants to do. As I have already said, nothing is simple anymore, not as simple as she would like to have it, anyway. Unfortunately neither she nor I can discuss our differences without getting excited, and the differences are so fundamental that they crop up all the time." There was real sadness in her voice when she added, "I wish it didn't have to be like that."

Quarshie remembered the local proverb, "If you think that a parrot cannot bleed, then look at its red tail."

When he spoke again there was a faint tone of compassion in his voice. He said, "Do you think Grace had any of the same feelings about your relationship?" Was there any sign that the girl loved her fat, grotesque mother, who lived by and for intrigue? was the question he had really wanted to ask.

Mrs. Artson-Eskill shrugged slightly and replied, "Who knows? Sometimes I thought there might be."

"And she is not in Grande Banane?"

"No. Not as far as I know. Why?"

"I received a mysterious letter suggesting that she might be. And have you seen this?" Quarshie gave her the newspaper with his picture on the front page.

She looked at it, screwing up her eyes.

"I can see it is a picture of you. What have you done to get yourself in the news?"

Quarshie took back the paper and read aloud what was written underneath the picture.

"Oh, my God. So it is out in the street."

"I don't think so. If they had had the real story they would have run it. No. I think someone is trying to make things difficult for me. I am going to see the editor when I go back into Port St. Mary. Did Grace have any contact with the *Evening News?* Or any of the other people we have talked about? Or any of those whom you deal with, or you employ, or anyone who might know something about your private life?"

Mrs. Artson-Eskill frowned, mentally thumbing through all the faces and names of the people she could recall before she answered, "No, not that I can think of."

"How about enemies?"

"I have dozens of them. Not only my daughter but lots of other people as well who will say that they hate me. How about you?

That story in the *Evening News* might be someone trying to get at you."

"I've thought of that. Hopefully I'll find out more about it from the editor. Now, there is one other thing I want your permission to do. May I look over Grace's room?"

"You won't find anything there. She lives like one of the servants. It's part of her way of underlining her rebellion against me"—she waved her hand to encompass the room and its furniture—"and all this. She lives in one of the rooms upstairs. You can't mistake it. It has almost nothing in it. I have been through the little there is there in case she had left anything that would help you." She wrestled herself to her feet. "I'll be in my office when you have finished."

Quarshie had not expected to find anyone upstairs, so when he entered the door nearest to the stairs he was surprised to find Rosebud sitting on the floor.

Her room contained a box, a sleeping mat and a mosquito net. Otherwise it was as bare as a prison cell.

The child was copying letters out of a textbook into an exercise book, using the box as a table. Even from a distance Quarshie could see that her penmanship was very uncertain.

Rosebud looked up with a startled, fearful look in her eyes.

He said, "I did not know this was your room, I'm sorry. Do you spend much time alone up here?"

"All the time, sah. I wait dissee bell dere"—she pointed to one over the door—"go ring. Den I go to moddah."

"And your writing is all you have to do?"

"Yessah."

"And if you don't do it?"

"Den moddah go beat me, sah."

Quarshie thought that though Mrs. Artson-Eskill showed some kind of human feelings from time to time it was hard to believe tht they had any roots in her heart. He would have liked to take Rosebud back to Mrs. Quarshie, so that she could be properly mothered and taken care of. However, he had to accept, at least for the moment, that it was something he could not do.

The child had risen to her feet when he came in and now she stood in a meekly correct attitude of respect. He rubbed his hand in the soft wool of the hair on top of her head and told her, "One day you must come to see me at my house in Port St. Mary. I will ask your moddah to give you a holiday small, small. Would you like that?"

The girl's eyes shone as she replied, "Yes, sah. I like it too much, sah."

"Good. Now you help me small. I want you to take me to Missee Grace's room, please."

"She no de heah, sah."

"I know. I want to look at her room. I have the key. Moddah gave it to me."

"Yessah."

"You like Missee Grace, Rosebud?"

"Ee be nice lady, sah." Adding shyly, "Sometime when she de heah I go sleep for her room."

"In her bed with her?"

Quarshie had given Rosebud the key, and as she opened one of the doors she said, "Never get bed, sah." And gestured to prove her point. "Missee Grace to sleep for mat, sah. I go sleep for her mat wid her, sah."

The room's furnishings were almost identical to those in Rosebud's room except that there was a built-in hanging cupboard, three boxes instead of one and an electric reading lamp on the floor beside the sleeping mat.

"Why isn't Missee Grace here, Rosebud?"

"Go away, sah, never go come back."

"Did she take any clothes with her?"

"No take anything, sah. All de heah for cupboard."

She slid the door open to reveal that the interior was closely packed with dresses. "Missee Grace shine too much sah," meaning that she dressed very smartly.

"Did she ever stay away like this before and never take anything?"

Rosebud frowned, thinking over her answer. Then, shaking her head, she told him, "Sometime she go one night, one night. Never she go for long time, don' take she clothes."

"Do you know if she has some men for friends, Rosebud?"

"She gettum."

"Any come here?"

"Dissee one work for dissee place here for town"—she pointed in the direction of Adaja—"come sometime. Dissee football man come see moddah come see Missee Grace after he finish downstairs.

Sometime odder man come one time, one time. No go come back. Das all."

It sounded like quite a parade. One which included Tete and As-teteompong.

Quarshie said, "Thank you. Now I am going to look at her things here. Do you want to stay or do you want to go?"

"Please, sah, I stay."

"O.K. That might be a good idea. If I find anything I can't explain you can put your sharp little mind to work on it."

"Sah?" Rosebud failed to understand him.

Quarshie said, "I go speak for myself." He opened one of the boxes and found it full of underwear and other small items of cloth-ing. "You go speak to yourself sometimes, Rosebud?" He asked.

"Yes, sah. Long time, long time every day I never get no man, no lady to talk wid. Mus' talk wid myself, sah."

As Quarshie knelt beside the second box he put one arm around Rosebud, who was standing close to him, and pulled her pliant young body against his. She melted against him and put one hand on his shoulder. He said nothing, and neither did she; nor did she look at him, allowing herself to take some of the comfort he wanted to give her from their physical contact yet maintaining a feeling of independence.

"Dissee box catch many book, sah. Dissee one"—she pointed to the third—"catch my paper."

"You looked at them sometime, eh?"

She was indignant and tried to push herself away from him. She knew he had intended to suggest that she had been prying.

She stopped pushing when she found he would not release her, and said, "I never get key for diss room, sah. I be here for inside when Missee Grace here. I see her go open dissee box, dat box, every box."

Quarshie said, "I'm sorry. I said something to vex you." And repeated, "I'm sorry."

Rosebud replied, "Yessah." And put her hand back on his shoul-der, from which she had withdrawn it to push herself away.

The books were a random selection. Quite a lot of them dealt with African subjects such as local literature, history, anthropology, cosmology, and so on. There were translations of French writers and one small bundle with an elastic band around it which inter-ested Quarshie particularly. It included works by Fanon, a man called Stirner (whom Quarshie had never heard of), in English translation, as well as books by Marcuse, Hermann Hesse and one or two others.

Glancing through the collection, he saw that she had the habit, which he had himself, of underlining passages in the text which interested her.

Once or twice, where he found that the passages were short, he read them.

From Fanon he read, "Let us waste no time in sterile litanies and nauseating mimicry. Leave this Europe where they are never done talking of Man, yet murder men everywhere they find them, at the corner of every one of their own streets, in all corners of the globe. For centuries they have stifled almost the whole of humanity in the name of so-called spiritual experience." In Proudhon she had been attracted by the simple statement, "My conscience is mine, my justice is mine, and my freedom is a sovereign freedom." Amplifying this thought was another that had appealed to her from Stirner, who had written, "Ownness . . . is my whole being and existence, it is I myself. I am free of what I am *rid* of, owner of what I have in my *power*, or what I *control*. My *own* I *am* at all times and under all circumstances . . ." Some words of Steppenwolf's that had particularly attracted her attention were, "For what I always hated and detested and cursed above all things was this contentment, this healthiness and comfort, this carefully preserved optimism of the middle classes, this fat and prosperous brood of mediocrity."

The last book he looked at was *One-Dimensional Man*, by Marcuse, and he noticed that she had bought it in Paris, in September 1968, and had made a point of inscribing that fact inside the cover as if it had some special significance. There was much underlining in the book, and amongst the many passages that were marked was one that fitted into the picture of Grace which was building itself in Quarshie's mind. The underlined passage read, "Technological rationality reveals its political character as it becomes the great vehicle of better domination, creating a truly totalitarian universe in which society and nature, mind and body, are kept in a state of permanent mobilisation for the defence of this (same totalitarian) universe." She had inserted the words in parentheses herself, as if to emphasise them.

She obviously had, he thought, a strong tendency toward anarchism, yet she was idealistic and fiercely against materialism. The anarchism probably originated as a reflex against her mother's domination, just as other aspects of her mother's ideas and way of life made her hunger for an uncluttered existence. Marcuse had spoken directly to her.

Were these feelings, he wondered, strong enough to make her want to punish her mother in some way, perhaps by disappearing and causing her great anxiety?

And where was the diary from which the excerpts that had been sent to him had been taken?

Rosebud, while he had been glancing through Grace's books, had gradually allowed her weight to sag more and more into his encircling arm. Now, as he put down the last book she stiffened again, and leaning forward so that she could look into his face, she asked, "You find something, sah?"

"Something," Quarshie acknowledged, "but not much. Rosebud, did Missee Grace write a lot in a book, maybe, or on pieces of paper?"

"Yessah. Plenty too much. All the time, all the time."

"Where did she keep the book, or the paper?"

"In dissee box, sah." She pointed to the one she had been looking at.

"Well, it's not there now, is it?"

"Missee Grace take um go, sah."

"When?"

"I no sabbee, sah. She no tell me."

"Too bad. Never mind. You have been a great help."

"If I help you, sah, den I be big with glad."

As Quarshie drove back towards Port St. Mary he thought of Rosebud being "big with glad" and Mrs. Artson-Eskill's bed that was strong enough to support a big woman and a big man. And he thought of the way such simple statements and unusual things tended to underline and reveal the tragedy that grew out of poor relationships between people and how much they all related to loneliness. It was a conditon that could be exemplified, one way or another, by each of the people he had contacted during his morning's work. A lonely little girl, a lonely older woman and a young one who was being forced into loneliness by lack of understanding, and suddenly he was tempted to be grateful to destiny, which had made him "uxorious" and had rewarded him for that quality in the return it brought him from his plump wife. He was also glad that the same destiny, which had started out by meanly denying them a son, had then relented and provided him with one he could adopt and who repaid him handsomely for all that his affection led him to do for the boy.

Mister Jwemoh, the editor of the *Evening News*, was a small man with eyes in narrow slits that glittered like black garnets.

"So, Doctor," he said, "you are one of those rare people who don't like to have his picture on the front page of a newspaper."

Quarshie looked very relaxed. In an unusually casual tone of voice he asked, "Whose idea was it to put it there?"

"Mine."

"What persuaded you it would be a good idea?"

"I thought you had been told."

"The mysterious character on the other end of a telephone who guaranteed his story with a considerable sum of cash?"

"That's right."

"There were no other considerations?"

"A front-page story about you helps the circulation."

"And if I insist that you drop the story?"

After a moment's pause Mister Jwemoh shrugged slightly and replied, "If you can convince me that it is harmful to your interests, or to anyone else's interests, I shall be happy to oblige."

"You will have to take my word for it that it does, as you call it, harm someone's interest in a case that may revolve around murder."

"But you won't name names?"

"Precisely. I shall also want to know the identity of your caller as soon as you have it. Has he paid the money he promised?"

"Yes. In cash. He sent it by hand. Of course you realise that what we have done breaks no laws?"

"Of course. I can take no legal steps to force you to kill the story."

"But," the editor said softly, "you have an uncle who is the Perm Sec at the Department of Internal Affairs and you also have the ear of the President."

Quarshie did not respond but sat quietly waiting for the man to speak again.

Presently he pressed a bell on his desk, and when a boy answered the summons he told him, "Fetch Doctor Quarshie a bottle of beer, one time. And one for me, too. We have just concluded an agreement, and it should be confirmed with the correct rituals. You will, I trust, drink with me?" he asked Quarshie.

According to the teaching of the spiritual lawgivers of our people, the most atrocious crime, the most ignoble and cynical debasement of the laws of nature, is the use of borigi in an act of destruction, whether this is effected by the use of sorcery or any other form of the evil art of witchcraft, by the naked force of a man's will used by one in whom it is strong when he is faced by one who is weak, or by any force a man may use to destroy the essence of another's being.

CHAPTER ELEVEN

"A dog will catch some animals, but it
will never catch a lion."

The note read, "Grace will be here, this evening, at my house. She says that you must not tell anyone else and that you must be here at six-thirty and bring her diary with you." And it caused apprehension to start growing in Tete's mind the moment he received it.

It had been sent by Wilson-Sarkey and brought by a young college student who had bargained over the price he should be paid for delivering it. He told Tete, "The professor informed me that you would be so pleased to get it that you would give me at least . . .", and named a sum that would translate into more than twenty dollars. He had refused to hand over the envelope until he was paid his "final" price, saying, "The letter is about Grace. I was told to tell you that."

Tete's immediate reaction was to contact Quarshie. When, however, after many attempts and a long delay, he finally reached the clinic on the telephone and found that Quarshie "no de heah, sah," he gave up, partly out of pique because the Doctor was not available when he wanted him and partly because he felt himself to be a fool for allowing the message to disturb him so seriously.

To a degree his anxiety was due to the fact that he did not have the diary anymore. Just the previous evening he had taken it down to the Post Office and sent it Registered Mail to Quarshie, which meant that it would be lost for at least three days in the bowels of the sorting office. Sending the document to Quarshie had cost Tete a great deal of effort before he had been able to make up his mind to part with it and to disregard Grace's fierce insistence that he should not, under any circumstances, share its contents with anyone else. When she handed it over she had told him that he was the only person she could trust with it and that if she left it at home her mother would be sure to find it and raise hell.

Now, in the early evening, he was driving north out of the town towards the University campus and his meeting with Wilson-Sarkey and . . . and he stumbled over the name even in his thoughts because he was suspicious that there was something false about the professor's invitation . . . Grace.

The news of her sudden disappearance had caused him to suffer a traumatic shock. Her reappearance, if it happened, would repeat the process.

He caught up with a line of traffic that was being held to a walking pace by a man driving a tractor. He was towing a flatbed trailer loaded with bales of stinking sun-dried fish, and Tete, needing some way to relieve the pressure that had built up in him, fumed against the "bush man" behind the vehicle's steering wheel. The object of his fury, the driver of the tractor, was almost naked, barefooted and oblivious to the animosity behind him. He was actually proud, delighted with himself to be sitting there showing off and shouting over his shoulder to the women and children to whom he had, with great magnanimity, given the privilege of riding behind him on his foul-smelling cargo.

The University grounds covered an area of five or six hundred acres, and when Tete finally reached the gates, over ten minutes late, he had to stop and ask several times for directions to Wilson-Sarkey's bungalow.

Then, when he finally arrived at his destination, he had the misfortune of thinking that the female who opened the door to him was a servant and said, "You mastah is expecting me. My name is Tete."

To which the gaunt woman he had addressed replied, "Yes, I know you, Tete. My name is Mrs. Wilson-Sarkey, and the master—that is, my husband—is in that room, and he is, as you say, expecting you." His discomposure reached its peak when Wilson-Sarkey started at once to treat him like a student.

In an obnoxiously authoritative way the professor looked up from a file he had open on the desk in front of him and snapped, "You're late."

Reminding himself that, as "the most valuable footballer in Akhana, if not in Africa"—an accolade he had been awarded by one of the newspapers—he was almost certainly better paid than the professor, Tete replied in a tone of voice that was as tart as Wilson-Sarkey's, "And Grace is even later. Or isn't she coming?"

When Wilson-Sarkey was evidently affronted Tete quickly followed what he saw as his advantage by adding, "If you are playing some kind of a game with me I suggest you knock it off, right? What have you dragged me out here for?"

The professor shook his head sadly. "No," he said, "this is not the right way to start a friendly conversation. Let me get you a drink. I have a bad habit of being overemphatic when I speak. I am sorry. It comes from addressing students and trying to pound knowledge into their skulls. Then it becomes a habit and I treat everyone the same way. Have a drink and let's relax for a little while."

"While we wait for Grace?"

Wilson-Sarkey took a deep breath, like a man about to dive into cold water, and said, "She won't be coming. To tell you the truth, I have not the remotest idea where she is, but I had to make sure that you would come out to see me. That's why I said she would be here."

It was information that, curiously, came as a relief to Tete, though he was uncertain why that should be. He did know that the feeling was something he should not show, so he leaned back in his chair and stared expressionlessly at his host.

He knew now that his earlier suspicions were correct: the man he was looking at was his enemy. So far as Grace was concerned, they had been rivals. Now they were enemies, and he felt the same violence rising inside him that had taken control of him when he had leapt at Quarshie. This time, he thought, the object of aggression was smaller than he was and a man with a second-rate physique. However, he repressed his instincts less because he felt that doing violence to the man would be wrong than because he felt that he would be making the move too early. There was some information he wanted before he gave the man the beating he felt he deserved.

He said abruptly, "I will have a beer."

"Good," the professor replied. "I was afraid you might say that you don't drink when you are in training."

He went to the door, and calling his wife, he told her peremptorily to bring two bottles of beer.

Tete said, "It is my doctor's advice that I drink a little alcohol now and then. He says it prevents me from getting too tense. He advises that I use it carefully and be sure that I don't drink anything but beer because, he says, in that form the alcohol is diluted and its contents even have a little food value."

"Who is your doctor? He sounds like a wise man."

"Quarshie. Doctor Quarshie."

Tete thought he saw the professor stiffen a little, but then realised that it could have been because his wife entered at that moment with two bottles of beer on a tray which bore no glasses.

Wilson-Sarkey told her, "Thank you." To which she reacted by turning her back on him, scowling at Tete and walking swiftly out of the room, leaving the air full of the thunder of her disapproval.

The professor said carefully, "Doctor Quarshie, eh? Do you think he is a good doctor?"

"He is more than a doctor."

"Oh? You mean that game he plays of being a detective? Do you take that act seriously? He seems to me to be a bit too much of an intellectual lightweight for anyone to think of him as anything but a clumsy bull of a man fumbling his way into and out of all sorts of ridiculous situations. He will find the truth of that one day when he comes up against someone with an above-average mind. A dog will catch some animals, but it will never catch a lion."

Tete did not change his position in his chair, or the expression on his face, but kept his eyes steadily on Wilson-Sarkey's. The man, Tete thought, is full of deceptive moves and devices, and he wondered whether that was his normal way of behaving. For a moment he made no comment, then he asked, "Why do you want to see me?"

"Because I would like to have that diary Grace left with you. It contains information I gave her that she noted verbatim, and it is material that is useful only to me, though it could be used by my fellow academics to their own advantage."

"You have no other reason for wanting the diary?"

"Have you read it?"

"She told me not to."

"But you did, anyway?"

"What would you give me for it?"

"Do you have a price? When someone asks that kind of question it usually means that they have some kind of value set on the merchandise, or whatever you want to call it, already in their minds."

Tete got up and went and looked at some of the titles on the spines of the books in the professor's bookshelves. "*Akana's Laws and Customs,* by J. B. Danquah," he read aloud; "*Wayward Lines from Africa,* by M. F. Dei-Anang; *The Religion of the Yoruba,* by Olumide Lucas; *The World Kinship among the Talensi,* by Meyer Forte; *Revolution and Power Politics in Yorubaland 1840–1914,* by E. A. Ayandele." He glanced along the shelves and added, "And several hundred more. Are there any with your name on them?"

"Yes."

"And you hope there will be others?"

"So you have read the diary?"

Tete had, in fact, no more than glanced at the diary and had found it too "intellectual" for his tastes, but he was determined to keep his companion off balance by refusing to answer his questions. "Why do you want it?" he repeated.

Wilson-Sarkey fought to restrain his temper. Taking his lead from Tete, he answered the question with a question. He said, "You don't have it with you. Where is it? In the car?"

"Pour my beer into a glass, will you? Or do you expect me to drink out of the bottle?"

Had Tete known it, this last calculated impertinence marked a point of no return in his association with Wilson-Sarkey. It marked the moment when the professor decided that he had no other alternative than to kill him. It was a decision towards which he had been building for a long time, one that he had been ready to make since he discovered that Grace's diary had been left in Tete's care. He had read the diary and started to make photocopies of some of its pages before Grace had found out what he was doing and had taken it away from him.

Now, he assumed that his visitor had read it, so, in Wilson-Sarkey's estimation, besides being an unpleasant and rude young man, Tete knew too much for the professor's and his own good. Besides, Grace had several times described Tete as unscrupulous at the same time that she had claimed that he was seriously in love with her.

Wilson-Sarkey went to a cupboard, took out two glasses and carefully poured them full, using beer from the same bottle for both of them. Then he handed one glass to Tete, held up the other in a gesture of a toast and emptied it at a draught.

Tete, as Wilson-Sarkey rightly thought he would, followed his example. As he put the glass down the footballer made a face and said, "What brand of beer is that?" He reached over, took the bottle and looked at the label. "Heineken. That is what I usually drink, but it does not taste like that. Where do you get it, perhaps . . ." A new thought came to him and he said, "But you poured both . . ."—his tongue felt as if it were thickening in his mouth—"from . . . the same . . . bottle. I saw you . . ." He tried to get to his feet, achieved this objective with awkward success and staggered across the room towards the professor. "You little bastard . . ." The words were slurred and spoken as clumsily as he moved.

He reached the desk and stood leaning on it, swaying, fighting to keep his head up.

Wilson-Sarkey came and stood beside him on his left side. He had taken a small black case and a rubber-capped ampule out of a drawer in the desk and was carrying them. With his free hand he took one of Tete's arms and draped it over his left shoulder, lifting against the man's armpit so that he was taking a large part of the footballer's weight. Then, with surprising strength, he manipulated the much larger man towards the door, half carrying him.

In the hallway they met Mrs. Wilson-Sarkey, and the professor told her, "Drunk . . . dead-drunk. No head for alcohol. I'm going to take him to his house. All that virility and he can't hold his liquor! I will be back in an hour or two. I have to pay a call on another friend on the way back."

By the time Wilson-Sarkey had the footballer settled in the front of the car he was about as sentient as a sackful of rice, though there was still a degree of hazy consciousness in his eyes. He sat slouched against the door with his head down on his chest, his mouth slack and leaking spittle that ran down his chin. In this condition he offered no resistance to the professor when he extracted a hypodermic syringe from the black case he was carrying, filled it from the ampule and jabbed it ruthlessly into his helpless victim's arm.

Afterwards he drove the inert footballer into town and in a deserted and dimly lit back street pushed him out of the car into the gutter, where he left him, and drove off back towards the University.

Tete was picked up about an hour later by a taxi driver who recognised him but failed to realise that he was not drunk. He took his passenger to Kwadoo because the big hairy man knew where Tete lived and could take him home.

Kwadoo's perception, however, was keener. He saw at once that

Tete was a very sick man and took him to Quarshie, who had little difficulty in perceiving some fairly evident clues as to what had brought about his condition. The indications, from the dilation of the pupils of Tete's eyes, the fact that he had obviously been vomiting, the faint but rapid beating of his heart, his high temperature and some subdued suggestions of delirium, were that he had probably been given an overdose of some drug such as atropine, which had excessively overstimulated his heart. This initial diagnosis was made more likely when Quarshie discovered the marks on Tete's skin left by Wilson-Sarkey's crude use of the hypodermic.

In less than an hour Tete was dead and the investigation, into what appeared to be a case of murder, was in the hands of the police. In handing the body over Quarshie made no mention of Tete's connection with his own investigations. For the moment any evidence he could suggest, or offer, could be based only on speculation and intuition. Also it might drag Mrs. Artson-Eskill's name into the investigation without offering the police any useful information on Tete's death. He himself had no evidence to show that the murder was related in any way to Grace's disappearance, though he would have betted his beautiful graduation certificate from McGill University against a bus ticket that before long he would find that, in fact, it had.

CHAPTER TWELVE

*"When you build a house you have to look
at many things besides the right place
to hang the front door."*

Mrs. Wilson-Sarkey said, "I can't understand how you knew that I
wanted to see you, Doctor."

Early the next morning, after Tete's death, Quarshie had set out
to visit both the Wilson-Sarkeys and Asteteompong. So his visit to
Mrs. Wilson-Sarkey had nothing to do with her needs—in fact, he
did not know what they were. He did not, however, disabuse his
hostess's assumption, but replied, "I came because I wanted to have
a word with you about your husband."

"Then you know where he is? That is what I wanted to talk to
you about."

Quarshie's expression maintained its serenity, but behind it he
put every faculty he had on full alert.

"Oh. You mean he has left? When did you last see him?"

Mrs. Wilson-Sarkey was not a very attractive woman. She was
boney and her teeth were so widely separated that they seemed to
spray out of her gums, pushing her thick lips out into a perpetual
pout.

"Last evening. He left the house with Tete. The footballer, you
know? The man was drunk, and the professor told me he was going
to drive him home. He said he would be back in a couple of hours.

"At what time would that have been?"

"About half past six."

"And you wanted to see me because he has not been home since?"

"That's right, and for other reasons. Come in and let me get you
something to drink. I want to ask your advice. I hear you are looking for the Artson-Eskill girl?"

"Who told you that?"

"My husband."

They moved into a room which Quarshie would have described as being too well cared for, obsessively so.

He said, "You keep your house beautifully."

Mrs. Wilson-Sarkey showed her teeth and replied, "Thank you."

Quarshie refrained from adding, "Because you are frustrated and have nothing else to love." Instead he said, "So Tete was drunk when he left. What made you think that?"

"My husband was half carrying him. Oh, I forgot. I offered you a drink. What can I get you? Tea? Coffee? Beer?"

"Beer? That would be very nice."

As she came back from the larder with a bottle she said, "This is what they were drinking last night."

Thinking of the condition in which he found Tete, Quarshie asked, "Were the bottles unopened before they started drinking?"

"Of course. Why?"

"How many of them? How many bottles did they drink between them?"

"Now that is peculiar, isn't it? They only drank one."

"Yet Tete was so drunk your husband had to support him."

"Yes, I know. I have only just thought of it. Of course, he might have had a lot to drink before he got here, or maybe he was suddenly taken ill."

Quarshie refrained from voicing the thought that came first to his mind, which was, "So ill that he died, of whatever took him, a few hours later."

Instead he asked, "And you have not seen your husband since?"

"That's what I wanted your advice about. What should I do now? There is more to the story than just that he has not come back."

"Then perhaps I had better know everything you can tell me."

"It is all rather complicated, Doctor. I must try and organise my thoughts. I had better start, I suppose, by saying that I am quite a rich woman. I have always wondered whether that was the reason my husband married me, though he always insisted that it wasn't. And, and perhaps you could help instead of the police if . . ." She was very agitated and seemed to be unable to concentrate.

Quarshie said soothingly, "Yes, perhaps I can, but why don't you just go on with what you have to tell me?"

"Yes, yes. I'm sorry. My . . . my husband has used my money to finance a lot of his work, you know, his digs and things like that.

Recently he has been spending more and more and . . . and yesterday he withdrew everything we had in our account. Actually, the only way I can control what he spends is to control how much money goes into that account. Part of the money he has been spending recently went on that girl you are looking for. They . . . they . . ." It cost her an effort, but she finally got it out. "They were spending the night together in hotels, quite often. He did not trouble to hide it."

"What about her?" Quarshie asked. "Did you ever meet her?"

"She is clever. Though I could never understand what she gets out of their relationship."

"Was she, perhaps, interested in his work? He mentioned the last time I saw him that she would make a good student."

"They go to Murder Mountain together. He has somethhing he is interested in there."

"What is it?"

"He would not talk to me about it."

"But if she went with him she must have known what was going on, wouldn't you say?"

"Perhaps." Then with her chin out she added, "Or perhaps they went there to copulate."

Quarshie changed the subject.

"You have been to a university, haven't you?"

"Yes, in England. I took a B.A. in biology."

But Quarshie did not hear her. His thoughts were elsewhere. He said, "Let me recapitulate. Your husband departed last night with Tete, who was drunk, apparently intending to come back, but you have not heard from him since. He drew a large sum of money out of the bank yesterday. He has found something connected with his work on Murder Mountain and he is having, or was having, an affair with Grace Artson-Eskill. Anything else? Why was Tete here to see him last night, do you know?"

"He didn't tell me. He didn't like Tete. I don't know why."

"Perhaps because our football star was also having an affair with Grace."

"Him, as well?"

Quarshie nodded. He drank his beer and stood up. "Now," he said, "I think the best thing we can do is to have a look to see if he left a message for you anywhere, or if we can find anything that will suggest where he has gone. Perhaps you have done that already?"

"No. I didn't know what to do."

"Where did he spend most of his time?"

"In his study."

"So why don't we have a look around in there?"

Mrs. Wilson-Sarkey opened her eyes very wide. She said, "Should we really do that?"

"Why not?"

"He never let me into that room unless he called me to come when he was in there."

"And you never went in without his knowledge?"

"He used to lock the door."

"Is it locked now?"

"I don't know. I don't remember seeing him lock it when he left. It would have been difficult because, as I said, he was half carrying Tete."

"Did he ever give you a reason for not allowing you to go inside?"

"He says he lives in a muddle and prefers it that way. People who live in a high state of order, he is always saying, are insecure, afraid that without the support of ordered surroundings they won't be able to operate. That little piece of criticism was, of course, aimed at me."

The door of the room was unlocked and it proved to be disorderly only in a rather superficial way. Below a degree of surface clutter the books and papers were carefully organised.

"What are you going to look for?"

Quarshie noticed the two used glasses standing on the desk but made no mention of them.

Instead he walked around the desk and sat in the chair behind it.

"I don't know. When you build a house you have to look at many things besides the right place to hang the front door. Everything here is just as he left it, right?"

"Yes. It must be. No one has been in the room since last night."

Quarshie picked up a file which was on top of the others on the desk. The label on it indicated that its contents concerned "Benin Bronzes." A glance through it told Quarshie that the professor had been collecting pictures and other details of sculptures which were created in Nigeria between the fifteenth and nineteenth centuries.

Clipped to the cover of the file was a newspaper cutting with a headline that read, "Benin Carving Makes $160,000 at Christie's."

"Does your husband have any of these sculptures?" Quarshie asked, holding up the file so that Mrs. Wilson-Sarkey could see one of the illustrations.

"Not that I know about. His main interest, from the archeological point of view, is not in African art."

Quarshie said, "The people of Benin made beautiful things. No one ever used that style or that medium, anywhere in the world, and did it better." He put the folder aside and continued to examine the other papers which littered the desk without finding anything else which interested him. Most of the material related to a lecture the professor was preparing on some recent finds in the region which had once been the scene of a great battle in 1240, when Sundiata had crushed his enemies at Kirina and thus taken the first step in founding the ancient West African empire of Mali.

Then he turned to the drawers and found that one of them was locked. To Mrs. Wilson-Sarkey, who was watching him, he said, "Your husband was rather a careless man, wasn't he?"

"Why do you say that?"

"He locked this drawer but he left the one above it unlocked. So" —and he suited his actions to his words—"all I have to do is to pull out the top drawer and then put my arm inside through the hole it leaves—like this—and fish down inside to see what makes him think that the contents should be kept secret."

Mrs. Wilson-Sarkey looked aghast.

She said, "He is going to be furious when he comes back and finds someone has been meddling with his things."

Quarshie shook his head and told her, "No. One of the advantages from the would-be meddler's point of view is the difficulty the untidy man has of being able to recognise whether everything is in the same muddle as when he left it or in a different one." As he spoke he was sifting through the papers he had taken out of the locked drawer. After a moment or two he paused and started to study some of them carefully.

Presently he said, "There is something which may be helpful here. Do you want me to see if I can find him?"

"Would you?"

"Why . . . yes." He said the words slowly, as if he were reluctant to commit himself. "That is, if he does not come back in a day or two. We don't want to start anything prematurely, do we?"

Mrs. Wilson-Sarkey said squarely, "I want to stop him running away with that girl or to stop him getting any further if they are off already. So nothing could be premature."

"I see. All right. Well, I want to make some notes from these papers I have found here. So perhaps you would leave me with them for a while. Yes?"

Mrs. Wilson-Sarkey looked worried. "What if my husband came home now and found you here like this?"

"Are you afraid of your husband? Or rather are you as afraid of him as you appear to be?"

Mrs. Wilson-Sarkey looked distractedly in any direction save directly at Quarshie. In a low voice she said, "He beats me."

"Why do you still stay with him?"

Mrs. Wilson-Sarkey looked at the floor in silence for a long while. Eventually she replied, "Why? Well, I suppose, in a way, it is because I am grateful to him. It is better to be used and . . . and even mistreated than it is to be ignored. To have no one ever know you are there, or see you, is like being dead." In a different tone of voice she said, "I will get you another beer and leave you in peace."

An hour later Quarshie had a sheaf of notes and had made another discovery, which, though circumstantial, began to give a definite shape to the suspicions that Mrs. Wilson-Sarkey's story of Tete's visit had aroused in his mind.

At the back of the locked drawer he found a collection of bottles and phials of drugs, including phenothiazines, barbiturates and several phials of atropine methonitrate.

When he had replaced everything in as near to the general order in which he had found them as he could, he took the two glasses outside and put them in his car, and then rejoined Mrs. Wilson-Sarkey in the living room.

When he entered she looked up from a newspaper she was trying to read and said, "Well?"

"There is no way I can positively identify what may have happened to him, but there are several interesting factors I would like to think about. One of them is how he comes to have a drawer half full of drugs of various kinds. It is the kind of stuff that should not be in the hands of anyone other than doctors, or druggists."

"Oh, he and that Asteteompong man are often together. That is where he got them, I expect. He's like a snake, Asteteompong. He insinuates himself into people's lives and then mesmerises them. He . . ." She was going to say more but decided against it.

"You have had some close personal experience of him, have you?" Quarshie prompted, feeling that that was the subject from which Mrs. Wilson-Sarkey had pulled back.

In a low voice she replied, "Yes. He experimented with me. That's what he told me he had been doing afterwards. I was a sort of laboratory specimen. My husband encouraged him and got full detailed reports of the results. I was sick with shame. He used hypnotism so that I did not know what he was doing to me, or what I was doing, until afterwards. They got together and persuaded me that what they wanted me to do would provide valuable scientific information about . . ."

Quarshie waited.

Mrs. Wilson-Sarkey shook her head. "I can't tell you," she said eventually. "I'm not prudish, or a frigid old spinster, Doctor, but I . . . I recognise some limits. Asteteompong said afterwards that there should be no limits to scientific experimentation . . . if one is in search of the truth." Then, bitterly, she added, "The name of the science they were serving was, I realised later, pornography. I am sure the world would be a better place without that man."

Know in your hearts, then, that the use of borigi is a wilfully sacrilegious act which only, through its corrosive energy, wreaks mischief against God's prime gift to man, life. Know also that it is "impossible" for there to be any fair reason to justify the use of borigi. It is, therefore, taboo, ungodly, unjust and inhuman.

CHAPTER THIRTEEN

The man . . . deserved to be dead.

A couple of hours later Quarshie found that there were other people who seemed to share Mrs. Wilson-Sarkey's view of Asteteompong and were not afraid to take their animus to a logical conclusion.

He had gone on from the professor's house to the sorcerer's house in Adaja. It was midmorning when he got there, and he found the bungalow and large garden surrounding it curiously still. Underfoot the mud was like thick axle grease, and on all sides the heavy shrubberies exhaled moisture into air that was already close to maximum saturation. It seemed that the plants were favoured over people because a man's sweat clung to his skin like a greasy sheath.

The front door was locked, and in the silence there was a suggestion of abnormality, even of threat. Quarshie also had a feeling that he was being watched.

However, when he looked around amongst the bushes of pink and scarlet hibiscus and the sodom apple trees which bear a fruit that gives colotropin, a heart poison, he found nobody until he almost fell over a man lying face downwards between two crabwood trees.

The unnatural way in which the man's bare feet were twisted inwards suggested that he was dead—a fact that Quarshie established quickly. Bloodstains, though they were slight, on the man's shirt led him to the discovery that the victim had been expertly knifed in the back by someone who had an accurate knowledge of human anatomy.

The wound was little more than a neat inch-wide puncture in the skin a fraction to the left of the spinal column and in perfect alignment with the heart. Since the skin on both sides of the wound was cut rather than torn, Quarshie assumed that the weapon was some sort of double-edged dagger.

Going through the dead man's pockets for something that would identify him, Quarshie found a key which, when he tried it, opened the back door of the bungalow. This discovery led Quarshie to the assumption that the murdered man had been an employee of Asteteompong's. He was apparently the only one, because the separate servants' quarters at the back of the house were unoccupied.

The back door led into a corridor which had two rooms on each side of it and terminated in a curtained archway leading into a big room. From the draperies covering the walls it was a room Quarshie recognised as the one Mrs. Quarshie had described.

The bungalow's owner was, in fact, still there seated behind his desk. There was, however, a difference. Like his servant, he was dead, slumped forward, with his head amongst the muddle of phials and bottles on his blotter.

Again Quarshie found the kind of knife wound in the man's back that he had found in the other victim.

For once Quarshie wished that he had the full apparatus of a modern criminal investigation section behind him, with a properly equipped forensic laboratory, fingerprinting records, computers, and all the complex paraphernalia that, in advanced countries, moved crime detection from being largely dependent on the ingenuity of an individual man to something approaching a science.

In the way he had to work it seemed to him that he always had to build his deductions upon an inadequate basis of certifiable facts. Everything was too speculative, as it was now, when he decided to work from the assumption that the two dead men had been killed by a person they both knew and therefore had no cause to suspect. For, Quarshie assumed, no man would turn his back on someone who was likely to be a threat to his life.

As he settled himself comfortably in a chair to think over the case, he had to start from the fact that two of the men he had suspected as having had something to do with Grace's disappearance had been killed in the last twenty-four hours.

Now, unless there was someone involved about whom he knew nothing, he was left with only two likely culprits, Mrs. Artson-Eskill and Professor Wilson-Sarkey.

It had to be extremely improbable that Mrs. Artson-Eskill would be capable of knifing a man in the back with that kind of accuracy

—though, he conceded, more unlikely things had come to pass. There was, however, no doubt that she could have hired a skilled assassin to do the work for her.

So far as the other suspect was concerned, Wilson-Sarkey's wife had given the impression that he was a violent and probably unscrupulous man, and there was already enough circumstantial evidence to suggest that he could have killed Tete. When he was able to get the residue in the glasses analysed, he expected to find evidence that would either confirm his suspicions or tell him he was on the wrong track. Again, careful perusal of the notes he had taken on the papers in the professor's desk could well provide strong supportive evidence that could make his suspicions plausible.

From the point of view of a motive for murdering Tete it did not seem unlikely that Mrs. Artson-Eskill might have had strong emotional reasons for wanting the footballer dead. And there might even have been a similar motive involved in Wilson-Sarkey's case, though, he felt, this was less likely.

Sitting there, facing the dead man across his desk in the bizarre, stagelike setting, Quarshie practiced a technique which allowed his imagination to free-wheel and to make random connections between pieces of information he had acquired that often led to unexpected insights and conclusions.

The curtains which surrounded him were pale blue and magenta. On a strip of bare wall beside the window and behind the lifeless body of the sorcerer was an extravagantly lettered certificate, issued by a British institute, which proclaimed that Asteteompong was entitled to write N.P.I. after his name.

From where Quarshie sat all he could see of the man was the top of his head, the spread of his shoulders and one arm flung wide along the desk top, with his hand clutched in a tight fist of cadaveric spasm. The man, he concluded, deserved to be dead. It was an unconventional judgement for a doctor to make, yet why, Quarshie wondered, should the human species be any different than other animals? When a creature became a threat to the health of a species, the other creatures would often instinctively remove it, or abandon it.

Could Grace be such a threat to anyone?

What constituted a threat was surely the key question. It would have something to do with the size of the threat; a major threat, or a minor threat.

His suspects, late and living, were all more or less selfish people, though all of them, with the exception of Asteteompong, returned something to the world for what they took from it.

Tete undoubtedly provided entertainment and a kind of catharsis by allowing his fans to release the bottled-up emotions that resulted from living in overcrowded cities. In effect his contribution paralleled that of the tribal drummer who beat the skins for dances.

Wilson-Sarkey taught young men and women to understand their inheritance.

Mrs. Artson-Eskill helped lepers and probably quite a lot of other people who came to her for legal and personal advice. Not all of what she had to offer would, however, have been inspired by feelings of disinterest.

Grace? She was still an enigma. Obviously she used her power over Tete for her own purposes, though she paid him in cash for any services she received. She caused her mother pain and unhappiness, but much of it generated from Mrs. Artson-Eskill's need to dominate.

What did Grace get out of her relationship to Wilson-Sarkey?

What did he, Quarshie, know about Grace?

She was physically attractive to men.

And she used that attraction to further her own purposes. What beautiful woman did not?

Even Mrs. Quarshie could be quite ruthless in the way she treated those who surrendered to her charms.

Grace had been in Paris during the student revolt in 1968. That was clear from the book by Marcuse which he had found in her room.

At that time she must have shared in the excitement of confronting the establishment, and she would have taken to heart a lot of the philosophy that went with the rioting and the baiting of the police. There would have been heated discussions around marble-topped tables on the sidewalks, with the air foul with the reek of Gaulois and with her face as distinctive as a brown egg in a nest of white ones. There would have been furious denunciations of France's ruling clique and the other politicians. There would have been adrenalin-stimulating street scenes filled with mob fervour and the belief that she and others were striking a blow that would benefit millions. As a way of life it was as addictive as the effects of a very potent drug and one from which it would be difficult to withdraw.

But how did all this affect Grace's relationship with Wilson-Sarkey? And was there likely to be any sort of relationship between it and the deaths of Asteteompong and Tete?

And what, if any, was the link between these last two events? Quarshie corrected the question: Not what, but who?

Either Wilson-Sarkey or Mrs. Artson-Eskill might fill the role.

Quarshie stretched and got to his feet. In a perfunctory way ignoring, almost contemptuously, the dead man, he started to search the room. For some time circumstantial evidence and his intuition had been shouting quite loudly and clearly in his ear that there was only one person he should be suspecting now, but he needed something more concrete than intuition to arrive at a final conclusion.

He found, as he had been sure he would, a variety of locked cupboards, which he opened with keys he found in Asteteompong's pocket, containing all kinds of pharmaceutical preparations, many of them no doubt stolen or purchased illegally from government dispensaries. Further investigation of this evidence of Asteteompong's activities could, he decided, be left for the police.

He next glanced through the hugger-mugger of papers that were on the desk and in filing cabinets. They were mostly dog-eared and dusty, and to a patient searcher they would probably reveal a more or less total picture of their owner's operations.

But Quarshie's intuition, in which he had greater faith than he would admit, made him thrust all the stuff aside impatiently for later perusal by himself or by the authorities.

One useful discovery was a number of phials of atropine of the same brand and dosage as those he had found in Wilson-Sarkey's desk. Though even this find was no more than another piece of circumstantial evidence because both brand and dosage were available, on prescription, from almost any pharmacist in Port St. Mary.

After locking the back door again Quarshie decided to pay a call on Mrs. Artson-Eskill before reporting his discovery to the police.

As usual he was greeted by Rosebud, who, he found, had a secret to share. She went about it as shyly as ever, saying, "Sah," and wringing her fingers down in front of her hips as if she were trying to twist them off, "las' time you de heah, sah . . ."

"Yes?" asked Quarshie encouragingly.

"You ask me ef I go ketch in my head som'ting Missee Grace go tell me."

"I did, Rosebud."

"Yessah. I go ketch someting, sah. Missee Grace do go tell me dat sometime soon she goin' be rich past all. Den, come dis time, sah, she go tak' me mebbee America." The child's eyes were shining.

"And you would like that, Rosebud, eh?"

Her voice was ecstatic. "Pass all, sah; pass all, sah." And then, "Was it good I ketch dat for my head, sah?"

Quarshie gave her two benis and said, "This is not for what you remembered but because you are my friend." And he cupped her head in the palm of his hand and pressed it against his thigh. "Now I go see Missus," he said.

"She deh for upstairs, sah," Rosebud told him.

When he entered the living room Mrs. Artson-Eskill said, "I saw you arrive. Come in. Come in and sit down."

"You mean you were looking out of the window?"

"No. But look there." She pointed. "I have a mirror placed outside the window so that from this chair I can see everyone who comes to the front door. I like to be prepared. I saw lots of mirrors like that in Amsterdam, and I thought them a good idea."

Quarshie said, "It's a pity you don't have mirrors that give you a view of other places besides your front door."

"Oh. Why? What have I missed?"

Quarshie sat down opposite Mrs. Artson-Eskill and, leaning forward, asked, "Where have you been this morning?"

"Right here."

"All the time."

"Yes. What is this? What has been happening?"

"Lawyers have a reputation of knowing where and how they can get dirty work carried out."

"Oh, for God's sake, stop playing around. Don't forget cross-questioning is part of my business. If you think I have done something, or employed someone to do something, why don't you ask me in plain language?"

"All right. Did you kill, or did you contract to have someone else kill, Tete and Asteteompong?"

Mrs. Artson-Eskill sat very still.

After a while she said, "You are serious, aren't you? In the back of your mind there is even a suspicion that I may have laid on this whole elaborate charade to cover up Grace's disappearance, in which you suspect me of playing some part."

Quarshie told her, "You said it; I didn't."

"Are Asteteompong and Tete really dead?"

Quarshie nodded.

"How did they die?"

"Tete was, I think, drugged, then given an overdose of atropine. Asteteompong and a servant were stabbed in the back."

"And you have evidence to suggest that I might have had a hand in these killings?"

"No, not a scrap. But you could have a motive."

"And you are trying the thought on me to see how I react. A device, I may say, that is an old one and fairly often used in the courtroom. And how does my reaction impress you?"

Quarshie shrugged. "As if you are armour-plated. Which is, I suspect, another spin-off of courtroom experience."

"In other words, I am not being helpful."

"Not very."

"All right, Doctor. I am going to continue to be unhelpful. You have suspicions about me. I am paying you and paying you well so I am not going to push you along any shortcuts. Prove your suspicions, Doctor. If you can dig up solid evidence, let's see how well we would get along facing each other in court. Eh? Go on, man, prove yourself, build a watertight case and throw it at me in court, and I bet I will make so many holes in it that it will sink without leaving a ripple."

CHAPTER FOURTEEN

"If it is good the goodness belongs to us
all, and if it is bad the badness belongs
to me, alone, who made it."

It was a familiar room and, for the Quarshies, a familiar situation.

They were sitting in the library at the French Ambassador's residence while the old man looked through the volumes of books, which rose from the floor to the ceiling all round the room, or hunted through his archival memory to find answers to the questions the Quarshies were asking of him.

Now, in reply to one of Mrs. Quarshie's queries, he said, "*Tu sais,* Prudence, there is a *fondamental* difference between the way most white men and most black men regard a misfortune. When we, all of us, think about it we mus' accept that the world is a very mysterious place, no? And we, *les blancs,* when something 'appen to us that come—how you say it?—out of the blue, we learn to accept it as what we call 'accident.' When something bad 'appen to us we may ask, 'Why has *le destin* or *le Bon Dieu* do this to me?' But we don't expect some answer to the question. For your people, most of them, there mus' be an answer. It is a basic *principe* of all your religion. In this, like in so many ways, there is contradiction, no? Your religion is much concern with the mystery of everything, but at the same time, it is very exact about cause and effect."

He looked backwards and forwards between Quarshie and his wife, who sat beyond the edge of the illumination thrown by the red pleated lampshade, so that only the whites of their eyes caught the light.

"So this bring us to the question in which everything begin . . . which is come first, the chicken or the egg? Religion or witchcraft? For me, I will say, the answer is that the expectation of an explanation for every accident open the door for witchcraft because some *malin,* some bad man, has see a chance to make naughty business for his enemy. I 'ave seen it wrote that witchcraft, wherever it 'appen, here, California, Brittany, India, anywhere . . . witchcraft she is the parasite of religion."

He cocked an eye at Mrs. Quarshie to see if his answer had satisfied her. When she nodded he continued.

"So, now, we can take a look at your dead witch doctor, the man, Asteteompong. When you phone, Quarshie, and say you want to know about this cult of Dagbata, I go to my bookshelf and, as you see"—he pointed to a pile of books on the floor beside his chair—"there is quite some piece of information available. Here is a little thing I find out."

He picked up a pad and glanced at the notes he had made.

"Number one," he told them, "Dagbata is come from the same region in Miwiland as Madame Artson-Eskill, and it is a very powerful cult. The most powerful cult, I think, in her country. And it is powerful because it was believe that it control *la petite vérole* . . ."

Quarshie took the cue he was offered to translate the French for Mrs. Quarshie. "Smallpox," he told her.

"Only the family from this Madame A.E. is more fear than this 'small pockets.'" The Ambassador continued, "One writer say, 'Even small pockets or thunderbolts, the killer fetishes of this land, do not make people so afraid as this family of the royal house.' It is a very important and clever family, you know? It have power over everything in the country, even the *'ochets,* the rattle which make noise to attract the gods. They could be obtain only at the palace, and it is told everyone that imitation will not work, so all people must hire his *'ochet* from the palace!

"Everywhere in Africa this god of small pockets is very big, very important and make everybody very afraid. Dagbata, he is call here, next door to Akhana. In Nigeria he is Shopona, and they sometimes call him King of the Earth and Lord of the Open, and they speak of a small pockets epidemic as 'hot earth' and the man who die of it is carry away by 'hot breath.' Even kings and big chiefs are afraid of its power.

"Dagbata, as a god, is also the giver of seed, of grain, and it is believe that when he is angry he can make the grain come out of everyone skin.

"Also, it is believe, because it is fact, that bad medicine with black magic . . . it is call *azondato* . . . can give this small pockets to people. The way they do this terrible thing is with a dead frog, a needle and a stick, which, when he is not use, stay in the frog. But when he is use the stick and the needle are take from the frog and are wash for seven days in the fluid from another sick man's small pockets and as well in the blood of a man who die from it. Also they make powder of the dry crusts that is take from the pustules." He paused, checked his notes and then concluded, "Now, to finish, I read a little piece from a paper that is from an American, a Mr. Frederick Quinn. He say, 'Death from this disease was the consequence of a heinous crime by the deceased, leaving a stigma on the family. Burial took place only with permission of the Earth cult's leader, not by ordinary gravediggers, but by a special team trained in and protected by magic. All the victim's effects were buried as well. Had the victim been a cult member, he would be wrapped in a shroud of red, white and black dots.

"'From seven months to three years after death,' Herskovits states, 'the family, after consulting a diviner, approaches . . . the cult with a ransom for the dead man's soul to his family. A wooden statue replaces the corpse at the funeral, and it is quickly buried with many charms.'

"So, my friend, you have pick a very big combination of forces against which you have to fight, no? A descendent of the royal 'ouse that is, not long ago, the most fear in West Africa and the priest, or black magic specialist, who is representing the most wicked and powerful juju. Did you find anything about this small pockets in the place where you find this dead man?"

Rather shamefacedly Quarshie said, "I did not try very hard. I will have to go over it all again. And Chobo. Did you find anything interesting about Chobo?"

"With this one you come very close to home. It is a good expression? When I am first here I make expedition to Chobo because I am interest in all this things, *archéologie, anthropologie* and *ethnographie* . . . and Chobo she is very interesting for me. So interesting that sometime, when the weather is clear, I look even now at her with my big telescope because once more they make juju there.

"And again you come to this thing like before . . . Chobo, Asteteompong. Madame A.E. are all hook together. The people of Chobo come from Mrs. A.E. country and Dagbata is one of their cult. They are like small *flaque*—puddle, no?—of stranger in

amongst another tribe. They are once run away from Madame A.E.
great-great-grandfather, or perhaps a grandfather with more greats,
who is trying maybe to make them slave and sell them to the English, or the Portuguese, or someone to take them to America. They
are very independent people, and maybe they are pain in the neck
for the King. So they run away to here—it is only about a hundred
kilometers—and this fine mountain, which is easy to defend, and in
this place they make their new home.

"And here, too, they make a place for their gods, and it become
sacré and, so, very important. Then is coming the British. By this
time there is many village around the bottom of the mountain, but
it is upstairs behind them that is the place where they keep their
shrines, their gods and the location where they bury their dead.

"Here, also, every year, because it is their tradition, there are *rituels inhumains* . . . How you say that, Quarshie?"

"Perhaps, ritual cruelties?"

"*Oui* . . . and also murder which are connect with their war
gods. When the British hear of this thing they don't like it. So one
time when a slave is sacrifice the British Governor come there with
a part of his army and he made a big palaver and say this *rituels*
have to stop and everybody have to leave the mountain. No more
fetish festival, no more puberty *rituel*, no more dead buried on the
mountain. And many soldier are leave there, for some come to
make certain all this thing 'appen . . . and they mus' knock down
all the village and town and *écraseé* all the shrine of the gods. So
the people had to give up the home of the ancestor and their
château, their fortress.

"Of course, she doesn't 'appen quite like this. Everybody is go
away, but after, secretly, they come back, especially the priest and
the cult leaders. And on special occasion when there are famous
ceremony is take place the chiefs and the chiefs of subtribes and
everybody is climb up the mountain to the sacred rocks where they
sit to make palaver and to the Murder Mountain, where murderers
are kill by a special priest and to the cave where the dead man is
throw afterwards.

"Today, after English go away, the place is . . . rewake. You understand. The priest of the cult come back and they hold their old
custom there again . . . I can see it with my telescope . . . though
it is only the old people who come back. Like everywhere, the old
religion is kept alive by the old people. The young worship the mo-

torcar and transistor, and the place where they go to worship is the disco. So, that is all about Chobo.

"Now, also you ask about Benin sculpture.

"So, I will tell you. Today amongst the cognoscenti this kind of art fetch money like the work from old Egypt and Greece, and it is my opinion that the best is as beautiful and *élégant* as this work from the eastern Méditerranée. It is possible, perhaps, that it comes —the style, you understand, not the work itself—from ancient Egypt. Something a little bit like it, you know, is call the Nok culture, and this come from a part of Nigeria more than two thousand years ago. Then it seem like the people from Ife pick up the form and make heads a bit more sophisticate but still something like the heads made by this Nok people. They are all terra-cotta. Finally come the Benin artist who work with bronze. So it is Nok two thousand years ago, Ife one thousand, Benin five hundred.

"Much of all this work is stolen and sold by black traders to white traders, and then it get to Europe and America, and every good piece can be worth very much money."

He put down his notes and asked Quarshie:

"Is it enough? Don't you want to know more?"

"I don't think so," Quarshie replied. "So far, in this business, I don't seem to be dealing too directly with any of these things. A knife in the back and an overdose of a heart stimulant don't seem to be directly connected to Dagbata, Chobo or Benin sculpture. Yet . . ." He left the word hanging, so that it was clear that he was avoiding the trap of drawing conclusions and having, perhaps, to say, as those who tell the traditional tales of Africa do, "This is the end of the story. If it is good the goodness belongs to us all, and if it is bad the badness belongs to me alone, who made it."

CHAPTER FIFTEEN

*"A lazy man's farm is the breeding ground
for snakes."*

It was late when Quarshie got home, and just as they were getting into bed the phone rang.

Mrs. Quarshie answered it and then turned to her husband and said, "It's a woman . . . for you."

Night calls usually meant agitated voices on the other end of the line. This call was no exception.

"My husband just left, Doctor." The caller sounded hysterical. "I must see you. He said I must see you."

"Who is this speaking?"

"Felicity, Doctor, Felicity. I . . ."

Quarshie recognised the voice and said, "Mrs. Wilson-Sarkey."

"Yes, yes, that's right. My husband came back, and now he has just driven away and . . . and he beat me again and left an important letter for you. At least he said it was important and . . . and he beat me when I said perhaps it should wait until the morning. He said, if you do not come at once I was to tell you that he saw you going into Asteteompong's house and then you would come at once. He was very upset, Doctor, and I am afraid he may come back. He wanted to know if I had sent you to Asteteompong's house, and told me he would kill me if I had. Will you come, Doctor?"

Quarshie frowned, and forcing himself to ignore his fatigue, he told her, "Yes. Perhaps you had better come and stay here. I will fetch you." He hung up.

Mrs. Quarshie was lying naked on the bed, and Quarshie sat down beside her.

She rolled on her side, so that her stomach was pressing against his back. Propping her head on one hand, she looked up sideways at him and asked, "Trouble?"

Quarshie stuck his jaw out and frowned. After a moment he replied, "I had a feeling I was being watched when I was in Aste-teompong's garden. It could be a trap." And he told his wife what Mrs. Wilson-Sarkey had said. Mrs. Quarshie shook her head. "I don't understand. How could the professor have seen you without you seeing him? What would he have been doing in that neigh-bourhood, anyway?" And then an idea dawned in her mind and she said, "He had just killed Asteteompong . . . and that man. Is that what you think?"

"Right. And . . . and what did Mrs. Wilson-Sarkey tell him, I wonder, about my visit to their house and my enquiries about Tete? There is nothing to suggest, or prove, that the professor has done anything to Grace, but Tete and Asteteompong may have known something Wilson-Sarkey did not want people to know. Now maybe it's my turn."

Absentmindedly Quarshie stroked Mrs. Quarshie's thigh with the tips of his fingers. Then, suddenly, he closed his hand tight, so that Mrs. Quarshie let out a little squeak of pain.

"Anyway, I must go," he said. "And forewarned is forearmed. Nobody is going to sneak up behind me and slip a knife into my back because I am going to make certain that there is a wall behind my back all the time. Do you want to come?" Then he answered his own question. "No. I am going to be busy enough guarding my own back. To have to guard yours as well"—he rolled her playfully onto her stomach and stood looking down at her—"when it is so elegant it might cause me to get distracted and to start dreaming of all the beautiful shapes I could carve that would have those curves for their inspiration . . ." As he turned away to get dressed he added, "Do you have any idea how beautiful you are?" And he left her with that question covering her like a silk sheet.

Mrs. Wilson-Sarkey was pathetic. One cheekbone was puffed up by a bruise, and her bottom lip was swollen and shiny.

"He's a difficult man, Doctor," she said. It was obviously a stag-gering understatement. "I sometimes wonder if he is sane. He knocked me down and knelt on me, on my . . . my chest, and kept hitting me with his fist."

Quarshie was embarrassed. With all his years in medicine he had never mastered the art of handling hysterical women. When she was with him it was something he left to Mrs. Quarshie because she did it expertly. He thought momentarily of her and felt a twist of hunger.

"Did your husband tell you whether he would be coming back?"

"No."

"And the letter he left for me?"

"Oh, I forgot. You said you were going to take me to your house, so I put a few things in a bag. I forgot the letter. It's here." She slipped her hand into the top of her dress between her breasts and pulled out an envelope.

"He told me not to lose it, and I didn't know where else to put it. He knelt on my back, too, and got his hands in my hair and banged my head on the floor. And he kicked me. All the time I kept feeling that he was afraid. What has he done, Doctor, to make him afraid like that?"

"Does he often get so violent?"

"No. He was always rough with me, pushing me, putting his knee into . . . up from behind me. He used to hold me from the back and do it and keep doing it. Then we both used to get excited and get into bed. I . . . I don't know what I'm saying, Doctor. What am I telling you."

"And he really went away?"

"I saw the lights of the car. He went all the way over to the campus gates and turned north, away from the city."

Quarshie opened the envelope.

"Get your bag and we'll go," he told Mrs. Wilson-Sarkey. Then he held the letter nearer a light so that he could read it.

The writing was self-consciously precise.

I am going to see Grace. If you want to see her, too, you had better follow me. I shall be up at the top of Chobo. Don't bring anyone with you. Come by day. You won't find your way at night. If you bring anyone with you they will probably kill Grace. She is due to be executed anyway. But I will persuade them to accept you. I can make them do the things I want them to. They are very jealous. Perhaps you will be able to make them see reason. They have people down in the village at the foot of the mountain, so don't bring policemen either. You must start from the village they call Degbe. In the past they had special men who could run up the mountain with a mes-

*sage faster than anyone else. Now they have flashlights. Don't
waste time. Executions take place at sunset.*

"And you don't know what your husband does on Chobo?"
Quarshie asked Mrs. Wilson-Sarkey as she came back into the room
carrying a suitcase.

She ran her tongue over her swollen lip and said, "Sometimes he
talked about being rich in his own right and not having to depend
on me for money. He was very positive about it, quite sure it would
happen one day. It was a great ambition of his to . . . to free himself of me. He was always working at it and scheming for it. He
used to say, 'A lazy man's farm is a breeding ground for snakes.'"

Quarshie saw now that she was crying. In an anguished voice she
said, "I gave him everything. I let him treat me like a slave and he
hated me."

Quarshie wanted to put his arm around her to give her some sort
of comfort but could not bring himself to do it, partly because he
was afraid the gesture would lead to a total breakdown and partly
because, in spite of his sympathy, he found her repellent.

He said brusquely, "Come on. We'll go and get into the car and
I'll take you home to Mrs. Quarshie. She will look after you while I
get in touch with the professor."

About an hour later he had persuaded Mrs. Wilson-Sarkey to
take a strong dose of nitrazepan and Mrs. Quarshie had settled her
in a spare bed in the room next to Arimi's and had stayed with her,
patting her hand until she had fallen asleep.

It was three o'clock when Mrs. Quarshie got back into her own
bed beside Quarshie, and she was surprised to find that he was still
awake.

She said, "If you are going to the mountain you are going to have
to get your problems out of your mind and go to sleep."

Quarshie shook his head. He told her, "That's not what is keeping
me awake. I have the next moves all planned . . . as far as I can
make any plans."

"Then what is troubling you?"

"All those curves I want to work into a sculpture." He reached
out for her. "I am not sure that I have the feel of them exactly
right. You wouldn't want me to make a mistake, or undervalue any
of them, would you?"

Know also and remember that all enmity, greed, envy, jealousy, evil-speaking, even false praise or lying eulogy, are severely condemned in the name of God by the spiritual lawgivers.

To any man who allows his greed or hatred to rise above his control the following reproach must be made: "Do you seek my death? Have you the killer breath in your heart?"

CHAPTER SIXTEEN

*"If you walk into the middle of a bush
fire you can't complain if you get your feet
too hot."*

In the morning it cost Quarshie considerable time and a lot of discussion before he was ready to leave for Chobo.

First he made arrangements with the French Ambassador. Then he spent some time with Arimi before he sent him, with a message, to Kwadoo. Finally he discussed his plans with Mrs. Quarshie.

She was the only one who argued with him.

"You are going to risk your life," she told him, "and for what? You don't even know for certain that the girl is alive. You suspected a trap when Mrs. Wilson-Sarkey phoned you. Why don't you suspect one now?"

Quarshie did not answer her question directly. "The man has borigi," he replied. "If I asked myself whether there was a chance that I might be infected by every sick patient I treat I would not do much of a job as a doctor." Then, with emphasis, he repeated, "I am fighting a man with borigi. That makes him more dangerous than a man with a plague, *tu sais,* Prudence?" He mimicked the French Ambassador. "People have to be protected."

"Who, Quarshie? Who are you protecting?"

"Everybody. Borigi is more than a sickness—it is an evil force. It can destroy society. And society is not an abstraction; it is a group of people. Arimi, that girl who came to us for help not long ago from your village, what's her name . . . ?"

"Ajua," Mrs. Quarshie supplied.

"Ajua and Dinah and . . . and that girl of yours in Adaja . . ."

"Edwia," Mrs. Quarshie supplied.

"Yes, Edwia and your sweet sister Patience, and, perhaps, especially Grace because Wilson-Sarkey has some sort of hold on her. If she is still alive. The man has become a killer."

"One who may kill you."

"I don't think he will. I know what I am up against." Quarshie managed to sound more certain that he felt. "Besides, I am involved now in a fight. You can't stop a fight in the middle and do your sums over again to see if you got your calculations right at the beginning. And if you walk into the middle of a bush fire you can't complain if you get your feet too hot. There are going to be problems, of course, but I have tried to anticipate them and to have the right responses ready to meet them. A lot could rest with you."

Mrs. Quarshie felt most unhappy. She liked to deal with the things at hand, and she was not sure that she knew what Quarshie was talking about when he spoke in abstractions.

What lay at hand was danger, which was not something her instinct told her to run away from, but she did not like to go into it as blindly as Quarshie seemed to be going now.

"But who are 'they,' Quarshie?" she asked. "Who is it he is talking about in his note? Who is going to execute Grace?"

Quarshie shrugged. "I don't know. Borigi gives a man the power to use others, or to make him think that others are using him if this furthers his aims. The thing which has got hold of this man is a kind of cancer. It is the thing which drives people to torture their fellow men, to commit mass murder, to invent things like napalm and the horrors that men have devised to use in biological warfare. It is the worst sickness in the world, and only men can be infected by it, not animals . . . which puts us well below other creatures in any scale which measures virtue." Quarshie paused and then concluded, "So, you see, the man has to be stopped, whether Grace is still alive or not."

To Quarshie it was as simple and logical as that. To his wife it was not at all simple, largely because her feelings came into the issue and confused it. However, she forbore any further argument, knowing that it would not move Quarshie away from his conviction that what he was determined to do was right, and she took comfort, small comfort, from the fact that if everything went according to plan, then her "feelings" would be unjustified.

As Quarshie made his way to the foot of the mountain, the evening storm swept in off the sea and thick cloud, weighted heavily with the burden of the rain it was carrying, enveloped the top of the mountain ahead of him.

From the French Ambassador he had learned that in the old days executions could occur only at the moment Dagbata was going to rest. However, they could take place only when he could still see and enjoy the offering which was being made to him. So executions happened not only at sunset but also when the daytime eye of all the gods, the sun itself, still could illuminate the ceremonies.

If Grace was alive there would be a stay of execution until the next evening because it could never take place when Murder Mountain was wrapped in the clouds.

Degbe, the village from which he had been told to start, was small and desolate. No more than six of the huts showed any signs of occupation. A dozen others were in various stages of disintegration. They were all roofless and stuck out of the ground like the sparse and crooked teeth of an old man. Even those which were still occupied had dismally ragged and unkempt thatches, with the ends that were nearest the ground making an uneven scribble against the cracked and crumbling walls.

Most significant of all, to Quarshie, was the fact that the village was without children or young people. It was as if it had been left to the natural processes of degeneration and decay, or else left to those who had spent most of their lives already and had nothing else to hope for except death.

Though he greeted the few old people he saw, no one returned his greeting until he was several hundred yards beyond the village and was at the beginning of the path which led up the mountain.

There, in the gloom made by the heavy cloud cover, sat a blind man functioning as, it seemed, a kind of sentinel. Though Quarshie was walking barefooted and making, in his own hearing, no sound, the old man called to him when he was still some distance off, "Who treads this road which leads to the region of the spirits? Are you one of those they have accepted?"

Quarshie said, "How can I be accepted by them, father, until I have asked for their acceptance? It is to seek their help and approval that I must climb to their sanctuary."

"A man who has not already had a sign from them and takes this path is foolhardy and invites their anger. They are jealous of their powers, those who rule up there, and will strike down those who step further along this path than it would be enough to break the strand of a cobweb."

"Father, I have business with them and with those who serve them."

"Business? What have they to do with business? Business has its place only amongst men. The gods live in the realm of the spiritual, which is as far beyond business as the sky is beyond the earth."

"Still I must go."

"Then the time you have chosen is bad . . . even the worst you could have picked if you had to live three lives instead of one."

"Why is it bad, father?"

"Because, big man—aye, I know you are a big man from the tone of your voice—because Dagbata is in a rage and will not be appeased. Our people here are afraid and will not even speak one with another for fear Dagbata will hear them if they say something by accident which will offend him."

"What can his anger mean to them, father?"

"That the hot breath will blow through the villages, big man. As it is already blowing on the mountain."

"What harm does the hot breath do, father?"

"It kills. It kills as fire does, without counting those who are the victims or whether they are men, women or children. Particularly it kills the very young."

"Still I must go, father."

"You sound as if you are without fear. Only a fool does not fear Dagbata."

"Then I am a fool."

The blind man shook his head and turned the pale grey marble orbs of his sightless eyes in the direction from which he heard Quarshie speak as if he hoped, despite his infirmity, to see him.

Softly he said, "That is not the admission of a fool but of a man who is overconfident. No others who have approached Dagbata with that attitude have had any more success than those who are, truly, fools. Go then, if you must. The path is marked with the shape of the human hand. You will not need directions for your return because . . ." And the man shrugged and left his statement unfinished.

A little further on Quarshie came to a fetish shrine. It stood under a sacred tree, an African rosewood which, when the bark is slashed, exudes a gummy substance that dries to a colour and consistency that is hard to distinguish from dried blood.

To an untutored eye the shrine might have looked like the scene of a gory ceremony, with blood liberally spattered on the small extremely simple thumb-shaped shrine itself, on the whitened rocks around it and on the various offerings and strips of cloth which hung from the boughs of the tree. In the past, Quarshie knew, human blood had been used to mix the mortar with which the priests had built their sacred shrines. It was utilised in this way not for any morbid reason—only Westerners find the shedding of blood morbid—but because it was the most sanctified element on earth, the material form of the human spirit.

Just beyond the shrine was a rock with the print of a hand on it in what might also have been blood or, perhaps, the sap of the rosewood tree.

Now Quarshie was faced with the beginning of the long continuous ascent of the steep part of his climb, and as he leaned into it, touching the rocky path with his fingertips, he thought he heard a soft fluted ripple of notes which were too well orchestrated to have been made by a bird.

The gloom was getting steadily more profound, and the atmosphere seemed to hover over the surface of a vast bowl of boiling water, with the clouds acting like a lid on a cauldron.

A little later Quarshie paused to rest and to look around him. Millennia before that evening the mountain had been made by a volcanic eruption. Now sparse vegetation had recovered it, but between the clumps of coarse grasses and other small plants, which grew in the shadow of the stunted, twisted trees, there were only the grotesque shapes of the rocks that looked as if they were covered with the rough grey skin of an elephant. Only the smoothest surfaces had resisted colonisation by some starvling plants or ferns. It was a spiritless scene which spoke of a struggle against the odds and the small returns won by even the most indomitable efforts.

And again Quarshie heard the faint trill from a flute, and though he could see no one, he suspected that somewhere out along the face of the mountain someone was tracking him and reporting his progress.

This suspicion was confirmed as he climbed into the thicker mists higher up the mountain and the flautist came nearer. Once out of the corner of his eye Quarshie thought he caught a glimpse of a crouching figure moving sinuously between some boulders over on his right-hand side.

He had passed several rocks marked in red with the palm of a man's hand, and he had to devote all his attention to watching the rock-strewn path ahead of him, so he could not spare much attention for what was happening on each side of him.

Once he thought he should adopt the same approach as the man who was tracking him and proceed as a hunter does, moving from cover to cover. Then he realised that it would be pointless because he was expected, so what could be gained from trying to arrive unseen? Despite the intense, steamy heat the clammy chill was beginning to seep through his skin.

The mist turned to the density of fog, and the notes of the flute were so close that he felt if he stretched out a hand he could have touched the flautist. The call the man gave had changed in a subtle way. Before it had obviously been a call for attention; now it seemed to Quarshie to be mocking him. And now, also, there were no identifiable shadows around him, only changes of the depth of the gloom which surrounded him, vague two-dimensional shadows which were always out of focus.

Then he thought he heard . . .

But he was falling and had heard nothing. Darkness welled up to meet him out of a vertical tunnel and the sickness of vertigo. "A brain lesion affecting muscular activity." Was he talking to himself or was his memory, or someone out of his memory, speaking to him?

While he went on falling he was powerless to move his arms or his legs. It was as if his skin had frozen into a steel shell, and his dominant need was to vomit because his stomach was filling his throat and seemed to be choking him.

Darkness is all, beyond darkness there is only darkness—it was a feeling, not a statement, and in the feeling the greatest part was fear. And still the steel skin held him so that he could not even twist within it.

If it was all directed towards the end, what would the end be? An explosion into light? Or disintegration? Still, these were not thoughts, but feelings. And then reason began to reassert itself and he remembered Mrs. Quarshie and Arimi, and he wanted to cry out to them.

The steel shell loosened a little and he could twist in it, and there was a coolness on his head and a voice said, "Don't fight, Doctor. Be still. Let the world come back, the real world. Be cool in your mind."

Quarshie opened his eyes.

The light was dim. Over his own face there was another. It was a woman's face, strangely painted with wide stripes of white running down from a cropped hairline to eyebrows which overhung what seemed to Quarshie to be the largest, blackest eyes he had ever seen. Along the cheekbones and paralleling them down to the jaw were more white stripes. Beneath the bottom lip were two other shorter white lines.

The eyes smiled into his and their owner said, "Hullo. How is your poor head?"

Other sensibilities came back, and Quarshie felt that his skull was cracked and that pain was seeping in through every fissure.

Thickly he said, "Terrible. Don't take your hand away." He closed his eyes. "You are Grace." It was not a question. "And I walked into an ambush."

"So you weren't unconscious all the time?"

"Not just unconscious but . . . but almost over the edge to eternity." He groaned. "You do the talking. Do it softly. It hurts me to think, or talk."

He opened his eyes again and moved them slowly, so that he took in Grace and her surroundings. A kerosene lantern stood beside his head; there were arching rocks above them and on each side; apart from the area reached by the light from the lamp there was total darkness. Gingerly he felt over his body and face with one hand and then he asked, "Talk. Explain why you are painted for a ceremonial. Why are you naked? Why am I painted and naked? Why are we both chained to logs of wood? And don't take your hand away." With his left hand he fumbled around until he found her left hand and took it in his. She returned the pressure.

She said, "Close your eyes. I'll talk." He obeyed her, and he found as she continued to speak that the tone of her voice pleased him. "It is funny that we should have come together here. Before I went to Europe I had what the English call a 'crush' on you. At its most extreme moments I would have said I would have been happy to die with you. I felt that strongly. I thought you were big and beautiful then—not stupid enough to walk into a trap to save me and get your skull beaten in."

Quarshie opened his eyes and found that she was smiling again. "You have been investigating my disappearance for quite some time. Wilson-Sarkey told me. I wonder what you think of me. No, don't try to put any words together. You told me to talk. Close your eyes. I'll start at random.

"I don't hate my mother. That's what everybody says, isn't it? I just hate the things which made her into the bitch she has become. That's why, when I am with her, I keep trying to break those things that fence her in. Inside she is as soft as I am. Or as you are, big man."

She was sitting on her heels. There were more white stripes painted on her body. Two ran down from her shoulders over the top of her breasts and down to her nipples. Three were painted downwards, one each from beneath her breasts and one in the centre between them from below her sternum to her groin. The double white lines were repeated on other parts of her body as well; only on her face were the lines painted in clusters of three.

She paused and Quarshie waited for her to resume, willing to accept what she had to say in whatever sequence she chose.

"I am trying to think of the kinds of questions you would want me to answer. I suppose my . . . my behaviour with men must arouse the Western side of your nature because, like me, you are two people, African and European—or is it North American? Well, my behaviour is prompted by both. What I do as an African, I suppose you could say, I do instinctively. What I do as a European I do thinkingly, consciously as a woman, a liberated woman. I use reason when I choose men whom I take into my body. I don't rule out whim, but usually if someone asks me why—why Tete or why Wilson-Sarkey or why Doctor Quarshie—I can give a reasoned answer. Tete, for instance, because he is so vigourous, and also because I was sorry for him. Somewhere along the way he has lost something. Wilson-Sarkey had—still has, in fact—something I want. It was the price he was to pay, or at least I thought it was. He has cheated me, like he tricked you. Which puts us in the same boat and is the reason I would take you." She released her left hand. "Will take you"—she touched him with easy familiarity—"if Dagbata wills it." He took her hand again and held it firmly. "No?" she asked. "But then that is not the only reason for, for coming together. I am beautiful . . . I am repeating only what other people say. You are strong, and I like looking at you because your face tells me that what I want to believe about you is true. So, Doctor Quarshie . . ." She left her sentence unfinished. "What else do you want to know? Doubtless more about the professor."

"Well, because my mother kept me so short of money, I stole some of the pieces of the Miwi sculpture she keeps locked away. I took them to Wilson-Sarkey to get him to give me a value on them so that I would not be cheated by the traders. He got an itch for me, and I helped him. I am good that way—it's a skill I inherited from my mother. She used to be famous for it.

"So he sold the sculpture for me and took his commission in bed. It was an arrangement that suited us both. There is so much of the gold, the carving and the other artifacts in my mother's store, all just thrown there higgledy-piggledy, uncatalogued, that I'm sure she'll never miss the few pieces I took. Anyway, I want the money to help people like that poor little slave Rosebud."

Quarshie opened his eyes again and lay watching her.

"I am telling you this so that you will understand. Before death confession is good for the soul, isn't it? This was what I needed. They have prepared me five times for sacrifice. Each time there were clouds. This evening, when it was cloudy again, they seemed discouraged, as if they got the message that Dagbata didn't want me. Then you walked in and everything was O.K. again. Dagbata wanted a double sacrifice, a man and a woman, that's the way they explain the delays."

"Why? Why are we to be sacrificed?"

"Wilson-Sarkey arranged it. From his point of view we are in his way, or we know too much for him to get away with what he wants to do. You, particularly, are too influential and too close to his heels, and catching up all the time."

"But by what power does he arrange these things?"

Grace shook her head. "There is a lot to tell you. I don't know how I am going to get it all said."

"And who are 'they,' the people he wrote about in the note he left me?"

"The priests of Dagbata . . . the surviving priests of Dagbata. He killed the others with smallpox."

"The hot breath?"

"The hot breath. Asteteompong had it. I mean he had preparations, a liquid which could be used like a vaccination and a powder which could be blown through a pipe. Wilson-Sarkey showed me the powder after he got me up here and he had already used it. He drugged them and blew the stuff into their nostrils. It attacks, apparently, through the mucous membranes. You'd know that, of course. There is a charnel house a little way down the hill and an old crone who looks after it. Their corpses are rotting away in there. The villages below have rumours of it."

"But why did he kill them?"

"There are two groups of priests, and their rivalry dates back to when they first settled here. One group, the traditionalists, the ones he killed, was against his disposing of the Chobo treasure. The others, the modernists, were seduced by the idea of not having to live here anymore and of having cars and, and everything."

"Treasure?"

"Yes, it came from Yorubaland centuries ago. The Chobo people came from your country—our country, you know? And before that, five or six hundred years ago, from further east. They brought a lot of Benin bronzes with them. Perhaps even the man who made some of them came along, too. It was all hidden away up here, and only the two priestly sects knew about it. They did not know it was treasure, though; they thought they were some sort of holy relics. Wilson-Sarkey told me the whole lot put together would be worth several million dollars."

"That's what has made him sick?"

"Yes, Doctor. Very, very sick."

"And he had to get us out of the way once we got on his trail. How did you find this out?"

"He told me. He was going to share the money with me."

"Then why are you going to be sacrificed?"

"Dagbata had to be paid."

"And Wilson-Sarkey made you the price?"

"Dagbata requires human blood. That is the only price that will wash the priests' consciences clean."

"How convenient for him. Two birds with one stone. How many priests are there?"

"About a dozen."

"And why am I to be killed? Did they tell you that?"

"Wilson-Sarkey did. He is very pleased with himself. He made up a clever story and they believed him. Once before, a good many years ago, the British drove the cult off the mountain. They left police or soldiers behind to destroy the shrines and the sacred villages. The African who oversaw all the destruction at the orders of the British was a renegade from the cult and the tribe. He had the same scars on his face that you have, so you come from the same clan and . . . and he was your grandfather. That is Wilson-Sarkey's story. Can you wonder that the priests believe Dagbata will be pleased?"

"It's funny. You sound almost exhilarated by it all."

"I am. At one moment. At the next . . ." She paused and then continued, "When I was alone I had too much time to think. With this log chained to my ankle—our ancestors were clever to use that idea instead of putting people in prison or lunatic asylums, no walls, no need to build latrines, the prisoner is mobile, he can sit in the sun, pound his *fufu,* but he can't run away or run after other people—with this thing on my leg I could never get down the hillside, and no one, except Wilson-Sarkey when he was here, would talk to me. I am taboo but I am not to be offended. If I die and I'm angry with them, I may influence Dagbata against them. I am supposed to be quite fatalistic about it all. Most of the time I am. I have been purified each day before they thought they were going to kill me. You will go through the ceremony tomorrow morning. We both will be cleansed, physically and mentally. The white stripes indicate that that part of the job has already been done.

"Isn't life strange? When I was in Paris I would not have believed that anything like this could happen. I used to watch the parade of fashion on the Champs Élysées from a café table—the elitists trotting out the new styles from St. Laurent and Maggy Rouff. Or I would drink my St. Raphael on the Boule Miche with Pierre, my boyfriend, and argue about the war in Algeria and the flics. And get excited about—what was that bastard's name?—the *éminence grise* out here, De Gaulle's representative, Fournier. Wherever he turned up there was always trouble, a *coup d'état,* a war. Pierre and I would plan ways of assassinating him. Then that was all so very real. Now . . . it is something written in a book and this is real. A naked man and a naked woman in a cave waiting to be ritually murdered according to a custom that is five, six, seven . . . who knows how many . . . hundred years old."

Quarshie thought of the plans he had made with Mrs. Quarshie, wondering if he should speak of them, and then decided against it.

Grace had made her adjustment to the probability of being

killed. It would be cruel to rouse her hopes of escaping if they might not succeed.

And he? He wished his head would stop aching and the bruise on the back of it stop hurting. He needed something soft for a pillow.

He asked, "Would you let me put my head in your lap . . . so . . . ?" He wriggled around, dragging the log that was chained to his leg to the right, relaxing back so that he looked up at her between the curves of her breasts.

Grace started to use both hands to smooth his temples and stroke away his pain. "Poor Doctor Quarshie," she said. "Poor man. You set out to save a damsel in distress and you wind up in a condemned cell with a nasty headache."

Quarshie managed a smile and told her, "Nonetheless, there are probably lots of men who would willingly change places with me. Not many condemned cells come equipped with anything quite so well designed to keep a prisoner's mind off his fears."

To summarise: every act directed towards the destruction of the life of others is called borigi, or the killer breath, because it is used to bring malicious harm upon the vital force of God in man.

Thus such an act is reprehensible in the sight of God, the giver and preserver of life. Since it brings harm to the natural order, to natural law and consequently to human law, the community has the right to defend itself against those who commit this act of superlative wickedness against any soul that has been generated by God to be a part of His creation.

The Book of Akhanian Philosophy
by
E. G. Astente

CHAPTER SEVENTEEN

"It is an easy death, Doctor Quarshie.
You won't suffer much."

"It is an easy death, Doctor Quarshie. You won't suffer much. Five hundred years ago our people were a lot more civilised than the people in Europe. There they used to draw and quarter their victims at executions. That often meant that while they were still alive they would drag out their intestines and then cut them up into small pieces. Except in cases of rape, or murder, we did not torture our people. We either cut off their heads or slit their throats. This evening, since the event is to be a traditional one, it will be the latter because the priests are going to need your blood to perform certain other rituals that will take place afterwards. It will all happen on a rock which juts out over a cliff. When the job has been done, your bodies will be pushed over the edge and will land on a ledge a couple of hundred feet down in front of the Rat Cave. The rodents and the raptors will then dispose of your remains."

Professor Wilson-Sarkey was still dressed for the lecture hall in his neatly cut suit, though, to Quarshie, his hair seemed to have grown longer and wilder. Also he was sweating heavily and his suit was stained in deep circles under the armpits and the patch pockets in front.

Daylight was pouring in through the entrance of the cave, and the professor had come carrying with him the aura of a surgeon making his rounds in a hospital. His manner was very unemotional and lighthearted. "You won't suffer much." That was typically part of the "jolly sawbone's" drill. "You know, I had not realised before, Doctor, how easy it is to kill people." Now his attitude was of one professional talking to another. "You just have to be sure that you want to do it, that's all. Once you are over that little hump you prick your target with a needle, or slip a knife between his ribs. Asteteompong wriggled a bit, as if I had tickled him, but that servant of his simply sighed like a very tired man and dropped at my feet.

"And your big day looks as if it has come at last, my dear." He turned to Grace. "You will be glad to have the renowned Doctor Quarshie as a companion in this great adventure, I am sure. Dagbata will be pleased, too. The priests can't get over it. It has simplified everything for them, you know. Got them off the hook, you might say.

"Oh, and I forgot to tell you, Doctor. Dagbata demands that you return to him as he sent you into the world: that is, without any possessions. So that ring on your finger will have to come off. Not now, of course, but later. The executioner can cut the finger off before he pushes you over the edge. Then I will get the ring from him and see that it is sent to Mrs. Quarshie. She will probably like to have it for a keepsake. You see, I am not a hardhearted man. I am sorry, very sorry, in fact, that that beautiful woman of yours is going to have to be upset. But she will get over it."

In the same matter-of-fact tone that Wilson-Sarkey had been using Quarshie told him, "You are mad. Do you know that?"

"My dear Doctor, what is madness? And who is mad? It is all a matter of degree, isn't it? A few percentage points up or down a graph. Those with greater intelligence than others run a greater risk of going beyond what people might recognise as the norm."

"And what do you plan to do with the money our deaths are going to earn you?"

"Yes, yes. I would say that that is a question you have a right to ask. Well, of course, there will be the Wilson-Sarkey Foundation at the University. And part of the terms of the sale will be that perfect castings are made of the bronzes—Grace will have told you about them—and they will be presented to Nigeria. Then I will finance more work by that man Leakey in East Africa. I consider it important that we establish this continent as the cradle of mankind. Wouldn't it be splendid if we could prove that it all started right here in Africa?"

"And your wife?" Quarshie thought of the pathetic woman he had left at his house.

"Oh, she doesn't need any money. She has more than she knows what to do with, already." The subject made him impatient and he turned away, saying, "I have to go." At the mouth of the cave he turned back and raised his hand in a halfhearted gesture of farewell. "I'll see you," he said, and walked out into the steamy sun-light.

Neither Grace nor Quarshie spoke for a moment or two, then Grace said, "It would be a lot easier to be afraid if it wasn't all so bizarre. I wonder what your professors at McGill would think—it was McGill, wasn't it?" When he nodded she continued, "What would they think if they could see you now, chained to a balk of wood, naked and painted and waiting to become the victim of a rit-ual murder?" Then with a change of tone she asked, "What is it like to be dead, Doctor? You have seen a lot of people die. You must know something about it."

"I am glad to say that none of them came back to tell me of their experiences. Most of our people on this continent have, I think, the right idea about death. No unbelievable heavens or hells for them. Their belief could be seen as simply as, say, a card being shuffled into a pack and then dealt into the world. At the end the card is slipped back into the pack again. It is all part of an unending proc-ess, except that we can sometimes choose who we are going to be the next time we come back instead of just leaving the choice to the dealer."

"Who would you like to come back as, next time?"

Quarshie knew that Grace was making an effort to be brave but that she was actually very frightened. He took up her game in an effort to help her.

"I would be a farmer with a nice fertile little farm where, most of the time, I could see the fruits of my labour. But no cash crops. The self-support thing with enough time off to . . ."

"To what?" Grace prompted him when he took a long time to continue.

Quarshie was sitting on the balk of wood and Grace sat on the ground in front of him, with her elbows on his knee, and he realised that the relationship he had hoped to establish seemed to be hap-pening. Curiously, she made him feel his age, which was just about old enough to be her father.

"To think and to remember."

"To remember what?"

"Amongst other things, the stories I was told when I was young. In them our people preserve most of their wisdom and their feel-ings about good and evil and their sense of eternity . . . which is that the life of the world stretches a long way back into infinite distances behind us and away out beyond the horizon ahead of us. No tricky beginnings or last judgements. They had a story to suit every occasion, to illuminate whatever was going on around them and to help them in times of need."

Grace dug her fingernails into the flesh above Quarshie's knee and said, "I am so very, very glad you came looking for me. I suppose it hasn't worked out too well for you, but for me . . . I was so lonely each time before it came to the moment when . . . when the ceremony was going to get started. The world was about to end for me, and everyone else was going to stay and enjoy themselves. Now it is just the other way round. You and I are going on ahead to find what there is there together, and it is all the others who are going to be left behind. Oh yes"—she put her head down on his knee—"I am so glad you came. Do you have a story for me . . . to help us in our time of need?"

"I think so. It's strange how our folktales, the same ones, spread all over Africa. It is as if when a story comes into being, the wind carries it from coast to coast. And . . . well . . . how about his one? There was once an age, at the beginning of all things, when there was no death but Man feared that it was coming. At that time the Moon sent an Ant to Man to tell him, 'As I, the Moon, die and dying, live, so will it come about that you shall also die and dying, live.'

"So the Ant started off on his mission. Along the way he was overtaken by the Hare, who asked him where he was going.

"Then the Ant answered, 'I have been sent by the Moon with a message for Man. She says I am to tell Him that as She dies and dying, lives, so will Man also die and dying, live.'

"Now the Hare is an impatient creature and a busybody, and he said, 'You are much too small and slow to carry an important message like that. I will take it.'

"So he raced off, and when he came to the hut where Man lived he said importantly, 'The Moon has sent me to tell you that as She dies and wholly perishes, so you will die and come totally to an end.'

"After that the Hare went proudly back to the Moon and told Her of the speed with which it carried Her message and the words it had said.

"Then the Moon was very angry because the Hare had pushed itself in where it had no business to be and had delivered the wrong message, and the Moon picked up a club and hit the Hare on the nose with it.

"Since that day the Hare's nose has been split, and some men have been foolish enough to believe what the Hare told them."

Grace thought about the story and then told Quarshie, "So, like the Moon, you are telling me that in dying we live. Is that right?"

"Yes, and I will illustrate the truth of it with a piece of history instead of a story. Not far from here the great Sefuwa dynasty came to power in the ninth century and continued until the last direct descendent quit his position as Chief of State in Bornu in the middle of the nineteenth century. So for a thousand years there was living genetic proof of the founder's immortality. The founder of the dynasty will also live on to the end of time in the history books. So, is he not immortal?"

"But I founded no dynasty, nor have I done anything notable that will make people remember me."

"Rosebud thinks you did. In her memory you are as beautiful and important as the moon. Her eyes shine when she speaks of you."

Grace sighed and said, "Thank you for telling me the story. I enjoyed listening to it. What it didn't say, of course, was how important it is to hope. I can hope that we shall in dying, live and hope that we shall be together afterwards."

The sun was moving down the sky towards the western horizon, and it beat on the ancient lump of lava which formed the mountain so that it became like a great chunk of fired coal that had not yet started to burn red. The heat clothed everything from the earth's surface to the covering of hazy sky, and at the same time it radiated upwards from the ground.

It was late afternoon, and since both Quarshie and Grace were to be offered as sacrifices rather than revenge killings the form the ceremony was to take was designed to allow them to keep their dignity.

Thus, when they were brought out to Murder Mountain, two of the younger priests carried the balks of wood to which they were chained to enable them to walk more or less normally.

Besides the priests of the cult and Wilson-Sarkey the only other witnesses to the event were to be the vultures. With uncanny anticipation they had settled on a crag above the small amphitheatre amongst the rocks, and with their black plumage, little ruffs of white feathers around their scrawny necks and bald heads, they formed a more strictly magisterial group than the men below them.

All the priests, and even Wilson-Sarkey, were now dressed in ancient bark-cloth robes and wore white hats which resembled inverted flowerpots. Except for the two younger men, who accompanied Grace and Quarshie, they all held the white clubs which would in the past have been human thighbones.

Of the men standing in the half circle surrounding the edge of the rock five of them carried drums, or had drums standing in front of them.

Quarshie and Grace were led to the edge of the cliff, where they were placed with their backs to the sea and the point of the horizon where the sun would set. There was almost an hour left before this would happen but, unlike the previous evenings, there was no sign of a storm brewing and rather than clouding over the sky seemed to be clearing, so that any possible postponement of the ceremony was becoming increasingly unlikely.

Suddenly, uninvited, Quarshie started to address the half circle of priests in front of him. They seemed surprised, but none of them interrupted him.

"Fathers of Dagbata," he told them loudly, "you have been misled into making this sacrifice, and I want to tell you for your own benefit that I have taken steps to ensure that if you proceed you will surely die the most shameful death of all, that of a murderer. You have been led into this error by the man who stands amongst you and is not truly a servant of Dagbata but a man dangerously inflicted with the curse of borigi, the killer breath. He pretends to be a believer in your interests and your taboos, but he is, I tell you, a deceiver, a killer. Nor is he satisfied with inflicting death on a man's body but, because of borigi, he kills all that is good in the world. Nobody and nothing that is of value, no child, no fruit, no truth, no spirit, can escape him. He is, at this moment, using you as his tools, and when he is done with you he will destroy you. So, if you continue with this ceremony . . . and the surrender of my life is only a small matter in relation to all that man"—Quarshie pointed at Wilson-Sarkey—"has done . . . then you will be guilty of unforgivable evil and you will not only pay with your lives but you will be judged before Dagbata and, even worse, before Him whose name we never speak." Contemptuously he concluded, "I have done with words. Know only that if you cause my death or the death of this young woman here you will suffer for it eternally because you will have defiled the sanctified gift given to all by Dagbata and, beyond him, by Him whom he serves."

In the silence that followed Quarshie's statement several of the priests and their acolytes fidgetted, and one was about to speak when Wilson-Sarkey shouted, "The man knows nothing and is telling lies. I know everything and speak the truth. Answer me, fathers. Did I not say he would come, and the way he would come, before he came? Did I not bring you the woman so that you could appease Dagbata with her? Did I not say that Dagbata would rid you of those who disputed your right to rule as you wished over the Nigerian hoard? Did not Dagbata send the hot breath amongst them, as I said he would? Am I not versed even better than you are in the laws and taboos of your people? Did I not recognise this man as a descendent of the pig who desecrated your shrines, raped your grandmothers and killed many of those whom they bore? What has he offered to prove the accusations he has made against me? Fathers, if after this man is given to Dagbata our god is displeased with me, I will accept his judgement and pay any penalty he may call for. And bear witness now to the fact that I call on Dagbata to multiply his displeasure with me by as many times as there are men here so that I may carry the load for all of you and thus absolve all of you from any wrongdoing. Is it enough?"

The Chief Priest said, "It is enough." And he gestured towards two of the drummers, who at once began to beat their drums. The first drum had a sharp, clear tone which resembled the voice of a woman, or perhaps a boy, and the way the drummer manipulated the skin made its voice sound like a human cry for attention. At once it was answered by the deep rumbling tone of the other drum, which spoke, at first, reluctantly and then with the dignity of an old man of great understanding and experience.

It was a litany, and it continued with requests from the light-toned drum being answered by the other, and the sounds evoked a drama that went beyond anything that can be produced by human speech. It was a dialogue, and it held all who heard it motionless and hypnotised as it built in dramatic force until it came to a sudden and complete . . . silence.

Then, apparently spontaneously, without a signal from anyone, all the drums together crashed into a sound that was sharper and more staccato than thunder. Overlaying this sound and audible above it there was a long-drawn-out ululation, a weird vibrating cry made by the priests in chorus beating their hands against their mouths as they produced one word, "Awo," extending the last vowel in harmony, but in a slowly rising scale.

As the first drumming had been cut off suddenly, so this unearthly cry and the rumble of the drums were cut off suddenly, too.

In this performance the first drumming had been a discussion between the god and his people concerning the need for his presence at the ceremony, and when he assented the second drumming and the ululation had been an African "Ave."

In the silence which followed, the Chief Priest stepped forward and began to lead the others through a chant of the ninety-nine songs with which all the still-served gods, their lesser kin and all those who could be said to have been shelved are remembered and venerated for their service to Dagbata.

While this took place the two young priests who had carried the victims' balks of timber came forward again. They were accompanied by a third man, who was very slim and very tall, taller than Quarshie.

In a practiced and expertly timed action both the younger men dropped to their knees and grasped Quarshie by his ankles. At the same moment the tall, thin man took the Doctor by surprise, stepping up to him and giving him a firm push. Unable to move his feet, Quarshie fell on his back, striking his head in the same place that it had been bruised the previous day. While his mind was confused by the arrows of pain which drove through his skull, Quarshie's wrists were secured in ancient cast-iron manacles and his feet were tied together with rope.

After the process was repeated with Grace, who offered no resistance, they were both turned so that they lay on their faces. It was mandatory that all approaches made to Dagbata, even in death, should be made backwards.

Beyond the coast to the west the bottom of the great radiant orb of the sun had just dipped into the sea.

The ninety-nine songs, each very brief, were coming to an end.

The moment appointed for the first cut with the knife that would sever Quarshie's jugular vein would be made at the moment when the last green flame from the setting sun, a phenomenon which can be seen only near the equator, flared momentarily above the horizon.

The tall, thin man, standing over the Doctor, took a knife, made from the blade of an old straight razor, from a small chamois-skin sheath. Without looking at it he held it across his body with its rounded tip in one hand and its hilt in the other.

Quarshie wanted to say something to Grace, something apologetic.

There must have been a miscalculation, or an accident, or some unforseeable human failure . . . though he still refused to believe such a thing. He wanted to make another protest, to convince the man standing above him and all the others that if he died they would all die as well, but the silence stifled him.

A fatal mistake must have been made, a truly *fatal* mistake . . .

And then the silence was broken.

Once again their were voices singing, but the sound was distant and the singers were women.

Quarshie's first concern was with how the executioner would react to this interruption. With a great effort he twisted over onto his back and prepared to put up whatever struggle he could.

The man, however, was staring openmouthed in the direction from which the sound of the singing originated. Painfully Quarshie raised his head to see how the others were reacting and saw something he had not expected.

Arimi.

The boy bolted into the middle of the amphitheatre and stood looking wildly about him to the right and left. Then he saw Quarshie and started to run towards him, but got only a few steps before he was seized from behind by Wilson-Sarkey. With Arimi struggling furiously in his grasp the professor moved towards the edge of the cliff shouting to Quarshie, "If anyone touches me I will take the boy with me over the edge."

At that moment there was a second unexpected intrusion.

Like a great, bounding black panther, Kwadoo leapt across the scene and brought Wilson-Sarkey and Arimi to the ground as cleanly as one of the great cats ever felled a buck. As Kwadoo got to his feet and Arimi rolled clear, the taxi driver had his huge hands in Wilson-Sarkey's hair, and he was trying to shake the smaller man like a woman shakes a rug. Then, with the same handhold, Kwadoo started to drag the professor to the edge of the rock and was about to swing him, like a sack of nuts, over the edge when Quarshie shouted at him to stop and at the bemused executioner to release him and help him to his feet.

The man had still not understood Quarshie and was looking at him blankly when the first woman appeared. She was out of breath, panting as if she could not possibly get enough air into her lungs, and her clothes were pasted to her body with sweat as closely as if she had just come out of a river. She was followed almost at once by several others, some of whom were not quite as exhausted as their leader.

Amongst them was Mrs. Quarshie. The women cut off their song the moment they saw what was happening, and Mrs. Quarshie, after a quick glance, had taken in the fact that Quarshie was struggling to his feet and that Arimi was sitting on the ground holding his head with a trickle of blood running down from a cut over one eye, felt that she needed some object upon which to release the tensions within her that had almost torn her apart.

She chose the Chief Priest, who was standing in front of the others, with his mouth open, as her target. She moved like a tornado across the smooth rock floor, planted herself in front of him and swung one hand through an arc of a hundred and eighty degrees to connect with the side of his face with a slap that sounded like a pistol shot and knocked the old man as cleanly off his feet as if he had been practicing an acrobatic exercise.

In her next movement she was on her knees beside Arimi, telling him that he was all right, that he was not badly hurt and that he had been as brave as a lion. Finally she reached Quarshie just as his hands were set free of the manacles and he could put one arm around her.

Between sobbing intakes of breath she said, "The last part . . . the last part of the hill . . . was . . . was too steep. Much steeper than we expected. I thought we were never . . . we were never going to get here. We should have been . . . in plenty of time. When I . . . when I saw the sun going down and . . . we still had a little way to go . . . I told the others to start singing. And Arimi and Kwadoo ran on ahead. Oh . . ." She clung to him tightly.

"It was a near-run thing," Quarshie said, not knowing that he was quoting another general whose reinforcements arrived only in the nick of time.

Mrs. Quarshie remembered Grace, and turned and asked, "Are

you all right? My, what a dance you have led us! You *are* all right, aren't you?"

Grace said, "Yes." She swallowed. "Yes." She shook her head. "Quarshie had it all planned, didn't he, and he didn't tell me. I . . ." She wanted to say, "I hate him," but realised that he had, after all, saved her life. She started to cry.

Quarshie asked his wife quietly, "How many women did you bring?"

"Forty-eight."

The Doctor faced the priests and told them, "There are forty-eight women and fifteen or sixteen of you. If you make a move to get away they will tear you apart." Then he pointed to a village three miles away across the plain. "And in that place there is a man with a glass which he uses to look at the moon. To him you are as close as if he were sitting there on that rock. He has police with him, and he can see everything which is happening and has happened here.

"The man with borigi and the hair, which he has grown to make him look unlike other men, will be treated like other men and will be punished as all men who commit murder are punished by the law. He is guilty of the death of many, for it was not Dagbata but he who killed those other priests with whom you disputed the right to dispose of the Nigerian hoard."

Now the tall man, who was still holding the knife in his hand with which he had been going to kill Quarshie, said in pidgin English, "What de go happen for us, sah?"

Quarshie looked at him, silently weighing his answer, and then told him, "The law he go fix you, too, my frien'. And every man, everywhere go laugh too much. You all big fool. Dissee man"—he pointed to Wilson-Sarkey—"go humbug you pass all. You all be like man he do go put he han' for crocodile mout' when crocodile he say he gettum gold dere for inside. Blood' dam fool pass all."

While Quarshie had been talking Mrs. Quarshie moved out of his encircling arm. Unwinding the top one of the three cloths she was wearing, she took it to Grace, saying, "You had better wear this." And, "I never expected to see you alive. Your mother will scold you when we get you down to her . . . She couldn't get up the mountain, though she wanted to try. She has not stopped worrying about you for one minute since you disappeared."

After that she went to Arimi. She wanted to hug him and pet him and make a fuss over the cut on his forehead, but she abstained, with a great effort. Instead she told him in a voice which choked a little as she spoke, "You were the one who saved your father's life. If you had not led us up the mountain so well and been so strong that you could go quickly at the end, we might have . . . we might not have got here in time. I am very proud of you." She had to grip her cloth on each side of her hips to keep her hands off him.

As the last of what she felt were the things she had to do she went to the tall man and asked, "Dere for underside dissee ting"— she pulled at his robe—"you get knicker?"

"Yessah, ma."

"Den, fool man, give dis ting, one time, one time or I fit vex you too much." The man's movements were almost panic-stricken as he scrambled out of his bark-cloth regalia.

Mrs. Quarshie took it from him, carried it to her husband and gave it to him wordlessly.

It was two days later, two days that had been filled with activity for the Quarshies.

All the market women, whom Mrs. Quarshie had rounded up to outflank Wilson-Sarkey, had been paid off. If squads of police or military had been brought to the foot of the mountain, the news would have been passed to the top with, probably, disastrous results for Grace, and perhaps for Quarshie, too.

However, since it was market day at Atimbi, one of the Chobo villages, an influx of market women was not regarded as sufficient to be considered worthy of a special report being sent up the mountain.

Kwadoo had been employed and handsomely rewarded to bring the women in a *trotro* from Port St. Mary, and particularly for his timely assault on the professor.

Quarshie had planned the last-minute arrival deliberately because he wanted the murderers to be caught red-handed. Nonetheless, the women were supposed to have been in position at least a half hour earlier. The actual climb could not have been started before it did because, again, a messenger might have been sent by Wilson-Sarkey's employees with plenty of time to warn him of the invasion.

Other matters that had been disposed of were first, and obviously

most important, the medical authorities had been told of the out-
break of smallpox in the region. Roadblocks had immediately been
set up around the mountain to control all movement in and out of
the villages and immunisation teams had been sent out.

Quarshie had returned Grace's diary to her—it had been waiting
for him at his clinic—without reading it. What it contained, he told
her, was no business of his as he had enough evidence against the
professor already. Their relationship was, at least superficially, cool
but friendly, and they found common ground in their concern for
Rosebud, who was delighted with the attention she received.

Quarshie's meeting with his employer, Mrs. Artson-Eskill, followed much the same pattern as all their meetings. For a change,
however, most of Right Honourable lady's acrimony was directed
away from Grace, or Quarshie.

The Doctor had reported on all the evidence that he and the
police had turned up against Wilson-Sarkey. It included the fact
that one of the glasses he had taken from the professor's study had
been found to contain traces of a strong opiate, that a postmortem
had confirmed that he had given Tete an excessive dose of atropine
and that a pair of shoes that had been found in Wilson-Sarkey's
house had been covered with mud in which there was evidence of
blood which belonged to the same group as samples taken from Asteteompong's servant. Another item was the discovery, at the University Department of Anthropology, of a typewriter with a type-
face which matched the type in the bogus *billet-doux* which was
supposed to have been written by Grace, in Grande Banane, to
Tete. The police had also been able to trace the messenger who had
delivered the money to the newspaper, and he identified Wilson-
Sarkey as the man who had handed him the envelope.

It was all this evidence which prompted Mrs. Artson-Eskill to
state, "The only thing that the prosecution is going to lack in
dealing with this odious little man is the power to hang him over
and over again for each and every murder he has committed. Perhaps our ancestors were right in making an execution for deliberate
murder a very painful process. Thank you, Doctor, for your services; you will have already received my cheque. Now Grace and I
can take up our internecine warfare at the point where it was interrupted, was it only a month ago? It will be interesting to see if either of us has learned anything during that time. Personally, I
would have some doubts."

Quarshie had also visited the Nigerian Embassy and told the Ambassador of the find of Benin bronzes, advised him that they had been transferred to the vault of one of the banks and that the Akhana government was prepared to enter into negotiations for their return to Nigeria.

Finally, the Doctor and Arimi had paid a visit to the French Ambassador, to thank him for his aid. It had been arranged that if Quarshie had been able to negotiate with the priests and to outwit Wilson-Sarkey he would hang a white cloth out where the Ambassador could see it quite clearly through his telescope. Then he would have sent the police in to arrest the professor. Since there was no white cloth it was the women who had had to be sent to the rescue.

The response Quarshie received from the Ambassador to his little speech of gratitude was predictable. His old friend had said, "That which I did is nothing. *C'était pas de grands choses.* That which please me most is the excellent behaviour of my adopted grandson." So it was left to Arimi to surprise Quarshie again, as he had on the mountain, with an unexpected move.

Speaking hesitantly but struggling through, he told the two men, "*Le fil faut suivre l'aiguille.*" The words were those of an old African proverb meaning that the thread must follow the needle, that is, he had to follow his father's example. It was a meaning, however, that had a double impact because the French words *fil* and *fils* can be pronounced almost identically, with the former meaning *thread* and the latter son.

Now, at last, it was bedtime on the third evening after Quarshie's near extinction on Murder Mountain.

The Doctor, on his back on his mattress, had been going over the case, carrying out a postmortem, and he said, at the end, "I have to be careful of my intuitions because they led me into doing sloppy work. I could have found, earlier on, more positive evidence against the professor but I did not because my feelings were so strong. First, I misled myself by getting the impression that Grace was already dead when we started out on the trail. Then, as I learned more about her, all of it to her discredit, I got confused about people's possible motives. Everyone was inclined to malign her, and I joined them. She is no saint, but she is a much better person than most of the other people involved in this case."

"Aren't there some people in the world, I don't know where they come from, who call her type a sexpot?"

Quarshie grinned at his wife's interjection. "She and I being together in that cave still troubles you, doesn't it? But it is what she is against rather than what she favours which makes me feel sympathetic towards her."

"What is she against?"

"Materialism, hypocrisy, unearned privilege. And then"—he returned to his earlier concern—"my intuition was roughly right about what would happen on the mountain. Roughly right," he repeated, stressing the penultimate word.

"Don't ever make it so 'roughly right' again. Shedding a bit of blood for someone may be acceptable, but shedding your life's blood, that's out . . . quite surely and definitely out," Mrs. Quarshie said.

After that they were both silent for a while, worrying over memories of what had been a traumatic experience for both of them.

Presently Quarshie said, "I suppose Mrs. Artson-Eskill will learn to treat her daughter like an adult one day. The ideas of the young are basically so much cleaner than those of their elders, even if they may be a bit impractical sometimes and blurred around the edges. The old, on the other hand, are too often willing to accept real dirt for the sake of expedience."

Mrs. Quarshie's thoughts also related to Grace, but they were a long way from being as philosophical as her husband's. She could not see Quarshie's face because he was lying with his head turned away from her. Then he turned towards her and in a lazy voice said, "Did you ever wonder whether what you are worrying about might be possible with both participants shackled to sixty-pound, five-foot-long balks of timber?"

Mrs. Quarshie lay back and in a somewhat mollified tone of voice said, "Yes, I suppose it might be a bit difficult." Then going on the offensive again, she said, "But you are not chained to a sixty-pound, five-foot-long lump of wood now, are you?"

"No."

"Then what are you waiting for?"

"For you to get over the suspicions that have been troubling you for the last two days and to inform me to that effect and issue an invitation."

"Oh. So we are going to be formal, are we? Very well, Doctor Samuel Quarshie, I have the honour to inform you, for and on behalf of your wife, Mrs. Prudence Quarshie, that you are invited to share with her a little . . . a little . . ." She hunted for the words, and Quarshie supplied her with them, "Nuptial bliss."